THE SECOND JUNGLE BOOK

THE SECOND JUNGLE BOOK

Rudyard Kipling

An imprint of Om Books International

Reprinted in 2019

Om Books International

Corporate & Editorial Office
A-12, Sector 64, Noida 201 301
Uttar Pradesh, India
Phone: +91 120 477 4100
Email: editorial@ombooks.com
Website: www.ombooksinternational.com

Sales Office
107, Ansari Road, Darya Ganj
New Delhi 110 002, India
Phone: +91 11 4000 9000
Email: sales@ombooks.com
Website: www.ombooks.com

© Om Books International 2017

Retold by Pooja Vasu

ISBN: 978-93-85031-86-1

Printed in India

10 9 8 7 6 5 4 3 2

Contents

Chapter One

How Fear Came

The stream is shrunk – the pool is dry,
And we be comrades, thou and I;
With fevered jowl and dusty flank
Each jostling each along the bank;
And by one droughty fear made still,
Forgoing thought of quest or kill.
Now 'neath his dam the fawn may see,
The lean Pack-wolf as cowed as he,
And the tall buck, unflinching, note
The fangs that tore his father's throat.
The pools are shrunk – the streams are dry,
And we be playmates, thou and I,
Till yonder cloud – Good Hunting! – loose
The rain that breaks our Water Truce.

The Law of the Jungle—which is the oldest law in the world—has arranged for almost every kind of accident that may befall the Jungle People and till now its code is as perfect as time and custom can make it. Mowgli spent a great part of his life in the Seeonee Wolf-Pack, learning the Law from Baloo, the Brown Bear. Baloo told him that the Law was like the Giant Creeper, because it dropped across everyone's back and no one could escape.

"When you have lived as long as I have, Little Brother, you will see how all the Jungle obeys at least one Law, and it will not be a pleasant sight."

The words went in from one ear and came out the other for the unconcerned boy who spent his life eating and sleeping without worry. But a year later, Baloo's words came true and Mowgli saw the Jungle working under the Law.

It began when the winter rains failed and Ikki, the Porcupine, told Mowgli that the wild yams were drying up when he met him in the bamboo thicket. Everybody knew Ikki only ate the best and the ripest, so Mowgli laughed and said, "What is that to me?"

"Not much *now*," replied Ikki, stiffly rattling his quills. "Do you still dive into the deep rock-pool below the Bee-Rocks, Little Brother?"

"No, the foolish water is all going away and I don't want to break my head," replied Mowgli, who was sure he knew as much as five Jungle People put together.

"That is a pity. A small crack might have allowed some wisdom in," said Ikki and ran away.

When Mowgli told Baloo what Ikki had said, he looked grave and said they must wait and see how the Mohwa bloomed.

That spring, Baloo's favourite Mohwa tree did not flower and only a few bad-smelling petals came down when Baloo shook the tree. Then, slowly, the heat crept into the heart of the Jungle and turned it first to yellow, then brown and at last black. The birds and the monkey-people went north, knowing what was coming. The deer and the wild pig went far away to the wasted village fields, sometimes dying before the eyes of the men too weak to kill them. Chil, the Kite, grew fat because there were lots of dead animals to eat. Every evening he brought news to the Jungle People that the sun was killing the Jungle for three days' flight in every direction.

Mowgli, who had never known what real hunger meant, now ate only stale honey scraped out of deserted rock-hives—black and dusty with dried sugar—and deep-boring grubs under tree barks. All animals were reduced to skin and bones, and Bagheera could not get a full meal even if he killed thrice in a single night. But the lack of water was the worst, because the Jungle People drank seldom, but deep.

The heat went on and sucked all the moisture, till at last only the main channel of the Waingunga carried a trickle of water. When Hathi, the Wild Elephant who lives for

a hundred years or more, saw a long lean blue ridge of rock show dry in the very centre of the stream, he knew that he was looking at the Peace Rock. Immediately, he lifted his trunk and proclaimed the Water Truce, just like his father had, 50 years ago. All animals took up the cry hoarsely and Chil, the Kite, flew in great circles announcing the warning.

By the Law of the Jungle, there would be no killing at the drinking places once the Water Truce had been declared, because drinking came before eating. During good seasons when water was plentiful, those who came to drink water at the Waingunga, did so at the risk of their lives. To cunningly and silently have a drink made night life fascinating because they knew that at any moment Shere Khan or Bagheera might make a meal of them. But now all the life-and-death fun had ended. Tiger, bear, deer, buffalo, and pig, all together — drank the dirtied water and stayed there, too tired to move off.

It was here that Mowgli came every night for the cool and the companionship. He was too thin to tempt even the hungriest of his enemies; his bones stood out like the ribs of a basket but his eye, was cool and quiet, for Bagheera was his adviser and he had told him to go quietly, hunt slowly and never, on any account, lose his temper.

"It is an evil time," said the Black Panther, one hot afternoon, "but it will go if we can live till the end. Is your stomach full, Man-cub?"

"There is stuff in my stomach, but it does not do me good. Do you think, Bagheera, that the Rains have forgotten us and will never come again?"

"Not I! We shall see the Mohwa in blossom again and little fawns fat with new grass. Come down to the Peace Rock and hear the news."

Bagheera looked at his ragged flank and whispered. "Last night I killed a bullock under the yoke. I am so weak that I think I would not have dared attack if he had been loose. *Wou!*"

"Yes, we are great hunters now," laughed Mowgli. "I am very bold to eat grubs."

Baloo joined them as they reached the riverbank. "The water cannot live long," he said, pointing to the beaten tracks of the deer and pigs that now resembled roads of man, lined with tall, dead grass. Hathi, the Warden of the Water Truce, stood rocking near the Peace Rock, with his sons. Close around Hathi were the deer, the pigs and the wild buffalos. A place was set apart on the opposite bank for the Eaters of Flesh — the tiger, the wolves, the bear and the others.

"We are under one Law, indeed," said Bagheera, wading into the water and looking at the place where the deer and the pig pushed each other. "Good hunting, all you of my blood," he called.

"Remember the Truce!" a frightened whisper ran along the ranks.

"Peace there!" gurgled Hathi. "This is no time to talk of hunting."

"I know that," answered Bagheera. "If only I could get good from chewing branches!"

"*We* wish so, very greatly," bleated a young fawn, making them all laugh out loud.

"Well spoken, little one," Bagheera purred eyeing the fawn to recognise him later. "When the Truce ends, that will be remembered in your favour."

The conversation continued but all news was bad.

"The menfolk are also dying," said a young sambhur. "I saw three between sunset and night, lying still, with their bullocks. We shall also lie still soon."

"The River has fallen since last night," commented Baloo. "O Hathi, have you seen a draught like this before?"

"It will pass," said Hathi, squirting water on his body.

"We have one here who cannot last long," said Baloo, looking at the boy he loved.

"I?" said Mowgli angrily. "I don't have fur to cover my bones, but if your coat were taken off, Baloo—"

Hathi shook at the idea and Baloo said severely, "Man-cub, that is not something to say to a Teacher of the Law. Never have I been seen without my coat."

"I meant no harm, Baloo; only that you are like a coconut with husk and I am the same coconut, naked. Now—"

Mowgli was about to speak more when Bagheera pulled him backward into the water with his paw. "Worse and Worse," he said, as Mowgli rose spluttering. "First Baloo is to be skinned, and now he is a coconut. Be careful that he does not break your head like ripe coconuts do." And he pulled the boy under again.

"It is not good to make fun of your teacher," said Baloo.

"That naked boy makes fun of good hunters all the time," said Shere Khan, the Lame Tiger, as he came limping down to the water. "Look at me, Man-cub!" he growled.

Mowgli stared back as insolently as he could and Shere Khan turned away uneasily.

"What have you done, Shere Khan?" asked Bagheera, as the Tiger dipped his chin in the water and oily streaks came floating down the stream from it.

"I killed a man," he replied coolly.

"He killed a Man!" started a whisper that grew into a cry. They all looked at Hathi, who did not react.

"I killed for choice — not for food," drawled Shere Khan, "and I have come to clean myself. Does anyone object?"

"Your kill was from choice?" Hathi lifted his trunk and quietly spoke; and when Hathi asked questions, it was best to answer.

"Yes. It was my right and my Night. You know, O Hathi." Shere Khan spoke almost courteously.

"I know," Hathi answered. Then, "Have you drunk your fill?"

"For tonight, yes."

"Go, then. The river is to drink, not to dirty. Only you would boast of killing now, when we suffer together — Man and Jungle People."

"What is this right Shere Khan speaks of?" Mowgli whispered in Bagheera's ear.

"Ask Hathi, I don't know, Little Brother. If Hathi had not spoken, I would have taught him a lesson, to come to the Peace Rock and boast of killing Man. Besides, he dirtied good water.

Mowgli picked up his courage and cried, "What is Shere Khan's right, O Hathi?"

"It is an old tale," said Hathi, "a tale older than the Jungle. Keep silence along the banks and I shall tell the tale."

"You know, children," he began, "that of all things you fear Man most. In the beginning of the Jungle, Jungle People lived together and had no fear of one another. There was no drought,

and we all only ate leaves and flowers, grass and fruit and bark.

"The Lord of the Jungle was Tha, the First of the Elephants. He pulled the Jungle out of deep waters with his trunk, he made furrows in the ground and there the rivers ran, he struck the ground with his foot to create ponds and when he blew through his trunk, the trees fell. And that was how the Jungle was made by Tha, according to the tale told to me.

"In those days, the Jungle People knew nothing of Man and lived as one. But they began to fight because they were lazy. There was plenty to graze on, but they wanted to eat where they lay. Tha, busy creating more Jungles and unable to be everywhere at all times, made the First of the Tigers the master and judge of the Jungle. The First of the Tigers also ate fruit and grass with others. He was as large as I am and very beautiful. There were no stripes on his golden fur and all came to him without fear.

"One night, there was a dispute between two bucks. It is said that as they spoke, one of the bucks pushed the First of the Tigers with his horns, and the First of the Tigers, forgetting he was the master and judge of the Jungle, leapt upon the buck and broke his neck.

"Till that night, none of us had died. The First of the Tigers saw what he had done and made foolish by the scent of blood, ran away. Without a judge we fell to fighting among ourselves. Tha heard the noise and came back, and saw the dead buck. But the Jungle People, made foolish by the scent of blood, could not tell him who had killed the buck. Tha then asked the trees to hang low and mark the killer of the buck, and then he said, 'who will now be the master of the Jungle People?'

"The Grey Ape leaped up and said, 'I will now be the master.' Tha laughed, and said, 'So be it,' and went away very angry.

"But the Grey Ape had only made a wise face and when Tha came back, he found him hanging upside down from the branches. He mocked those below him and they mocked him in return and thus there was no Law in the Jungle, only foolish talk and senseless words.

"Then Tha called everyone and said, 'The first of your masters has brought Death and the second has brought Shame to the Jungle. But now you shall have a Law that you must not break. Now you shall know Fear, and when you have found him, you shall know that he is your master.'

"The Jungle People went everywhere seeking Fear, until the buffaloes came back with news that in a cave in the Jungle sat Fear, and that he had no hair and went on his hind legs. Everyone went to the cave to find Fear at the mouth of the cave, hairless and standing on his hind legs. He cried out and his voice filled everyone with fear. That night, for the first time, they did not sleep as one, but according to tribes.

"Only the First of the Tigers was missing and when word of the Thing at the cave reached him in the marshes of the North, he decided to go and break his neck. As he ran through the night, the trees and creepers on his path remembered Tha's orders and marked him as he ran. They left stripes on his yellow fur.

"He reached the cave where Fear saw him and called to him but he was afraid and ran away, howling.

"When Tha heard the howling, he found him and asked what the sorrow was. The First of the Tigers replied that he was ashamed as he had run away from the Hairless One, and he had also been called a shameful name because he was smeared with the mud of the marshes. He tried to wash away the stripes, but not a bar changed. Tha saw this and laughed, 'You have let Death loose upon the Jungle, and with Death comes Fear. The People of the Jungle are afraid of you and you are afraid of the Hairless One.'

27

" 'They will never fear me, for I have known them since the beginning,' said the First of the Tigers and ran calling out to the Jungle People. They all ran away from him, for they were afraid.

"He came back to Tha and begged not to be forgotten, to let his children remember that he was once without the shame of Fear. Tha agreed to that and said that for one night every year, all would be as it had been before he had killed the buck, for him and his children. That he would not be afraid of the Hairless One, called Man, but that Man would be afraid of him. 'Show him, mercy in that night of fear, for you have known what fear is.'

"The First of the Tigers answered, 'I am content.' But a little while later, as he drank, he saw the black stripes and remembered the name Man had called him and was angry. He waited for a year in the marshes till the night Tha had promised him. He then went to the cave and just as Tha had promised, Man lay along the

ground in fear in front of him. The First of the tigers struck him, breaking his back and killing him. He thought that he was the only Man and that he had killed Fear.

"When Tha saw what the First of the Tigers had done, he asked, 'Is this mercy?'

"When the First of the Tigers replied that it did not matter, for he had killed Fear, Tha said, 'O blind and foolish! You have untied the feet of Death and he will follow you till the day you die. You have taught Man to kill!'

"And Tha continued, 'Never again shall the Jungle people cross your path, only Fear will follow you. He will make the grounds open below you, the creepers to twist around your neck and the tree trunks to grow together higher than you can leap. At last he will take your skin and wrap his cubs when they are cold. You showed him no mercy and none will he show you.'

"Still bold from the night, the First of the Tigers told Tha that he had promised him one night of no Fear and must not take it away. Tha agreed but said that there was price to pay. 'You have taught Man to kill and he is a fast learner.'

"When day came, another Hairless One came out of the cave and saw the kill and the First of the Tigers standing over it. He threw a pointed stick which struck the First of the Tigers deep in the flank. He ran through the Jungle howling in pain until he got rid of the stick and everyone who heard him knew that Man could hit from far and were even more afraid.

"And you know the harm Man has done to all our People since then. Yet, for one night of each year, he fears the Tiger, as Tha had promised. In this one night, Tiger kills Man, remembering how the First of the Tigers was made ashamed."

"But Shere Khan kills Man twice or thrice in a month," said Mowgli.

"Yes," replied Tha, "but then he springs from behind, full of fear. On this one night, he walks to their houses and kills as they fall on their faces in front of him."

"Oh! That's why he asked me to look at him! But I did not fall at his feet, since I am not Man, but one of Free People."

"Do the men know this—tale?" asked Bagheera, smiling wickedly.

"Only the Tigers and the children of Tha knew it. Now all of you by the pool have heard it too."

Hathi dipped his trunk in the water indicating that he did not wish to talk anymore.

"But," said Mowgli, turning to Baloo, "why did the First of the Tigers stop eating grass and leaves? He had only broken the buck's neck. Why did he start eating meat?"

"The trees and creepers had marked him, Little Brother. He would never again eat their fruits, but only avenge himself upon the Eaters of Grass," said Baloo.

"Then you knew the tale. Why did you not tell me?" asked Mowgli.

"Because the Jungle is full of such tales and if I began there would be no end to them. Let go of my ear, Little Brother."

The law of the jungle

Just to give you an idea of the immense variety of the Jungle Law, I have translated into verse a few that apply to the wolves. Baloo always sang them in a singsong. There are hundreds more but these will do for simpler rulings.

Now this is the Law of the Jungle – as old and as true as the sky;
And the Wolf that shall keep it may prosper, but the Wolf
*   that shall break it must die.*

As the creeper that girdles the tree-trunk the Law runs
*   forward and back –*
For the strength of the Pack is the Wolf, and the strength of
*   the Wolf is the Pack.*

Wash daily from nose-tip to tail-tip; drink deeply, but
    never too deep;
And remember the night is for hunting, and forget not
    the day is for sleep.

The Jackal may follow the tiger, but, Cub, when thy
    whiskers are grown,
Remember the Wold is a hunter — go forth and get food
    of thine own.

Keep peace with the Lords of the Jungle — the Tiger, the
    Panther, the Bear;
And trouble not Hathi the Silent, and mock not the
    boar in his lair.

When Pack meets with the Pack in the Jungle, and
    neither will go with the trail,
Lie down till the leaders have spoken — it may be fair
    words shall prevail.

When ye fight with a Wolf of the Pack, ye must fight
    him alone and afar,
Lest others take part in the quarrel, and the Pack be
    diminished by war.

The Lair of the Wolf is his refuge, but where he has dug
    it too plain,
The Council shall send him a message, and so he shall
    change it again.

If ye kill for yourselves, and your mates, and your cubs
    as they need, and ye can;
But not kill for pleasure if killing and *seven times never
    kill Man.*

If ye plunder his kill from a weaker, devour not all in
thy pride;
Pack-Right is the right of the meanest; so leave him the
head and the hide.

The Kill of the Pack is the meat of the Pack. Ye must eat
where it lies;
And no one may carry away that meat to his lair, or he
dies.

The kill of the Wolf is the meat of the Wolf. He may do
what he will,
But, till he has given permission, the Pack may not eat
of that kill.

Cub-Right is the right of the Yearling. From all of his
Pack he may claim
Fill-gorge when the killer has eaten; and none may
refuse him the same.

Lair-Right is the right of the Mother. From all of her
year she may claim
One haunch of each kill for her litter, and none may
deny her the same.

Cave-Right is the right of the Father — to hunt by
himself for his own.
He is free of all calls to the Pack; he is judged by the
Council alone.

Because of his age and his cunning, because of his gripe
and his paw,
In all that the law leaves open, the word of the Head
Wolf is Law.

*Now these are the Laws of the Jungle, and many and mighty
are they;*
*But the head and the hoof of the Law and the haunch and the
hump is – Obey!*

Chapter Two

The Miracle of Purun Bhagat

The night we felt the earth would move
We stole and plucked him by the hand,
Because we loved him with the love
That knows but cannot understand.

And when the roaring hillside broke,
And all our world fell down in rain,
We saved him, we the Little Folk;
But lo! He does not come again!

Mourn now, we saved him for the sake
Of such poor love as wild ones may.
Mourn ye! Our brother will not wake,
And his own kind drive us away!

There was once a man in India who was the Prime Minister of one of the semi-independent native states in the north-western part of the country. He was a Brahmin of such high caste that caste had no meaning for him. His father had been an important official in the old-fashioned Hindu Court. But as Purun Dass grew up he felt that the old ways were changing and that if anyone wanted to get on in the world he must stand well with the British and imitate the ways they thought were good. At the same time, it was important that the favour of the Indian Masters was not lost. This was a difficult game, but the quiet young Brahmin, helped by an English education at the Bombay University, played it cool and slowly rose to be the Prime Minister of the kingdom. He held more power than his master, the Maharajah.

The old king — suspicious of the English and their railways and telegraphs — died and Purun Dass stood high with the young successor who had been taught by an Englishman. Between them, taking care that the master always got the credit, they established schools for little girls, made roads, started state dispensaries and shows of agricultural implements and published a yearly blue-book on the 'Moral and Material Progress of the State,' delighting the Foreign Office and the Government of India. Very few native states took up English progress, unwilling to believe as Purun Dass showed he did, that what was good for the Englishman must be twice as good for the Asiatic. The Prime Minister became an honoured friend of Viceroys, and Governors and Lieutenant-Governors and medical missionaries, and common missionaries and hard-riding English Officers who came to shoot in the State preserves and hosts of tourists who travelled up and down India in cold weather, showing how things ought to be managed. In his spare time, he would endow scholarships for the study of medicine and manufactures on English lines, and write letters to the *Pioneer*, the greatest Indian daily paper, explaining his master's aims and objects.

When he finally visited England, he paid enormous sums to the priests on his return because he had lost his caste on crossing the Black Sea. In London, he met with everyone worth knowing and was given honorary degrees by learned universities. He talked about Hindu Social reforms and made speeches until all London declared that he was the most fascinating man they had ever met. When he returned to India, he received a grand welcome and the Viceroy himself made a special visit to shower him with riches. He made Purun Dass the Knight Commander of the Indian Empire and that evening at dinner Purun Dass made a speech which few Englishmen could have bettered.

But next month, he did something no Englishman would have dreamed of doing

because as far as the world's affairs were concerned, he died. Purun Dass resigned from his position of power, gave up everything and took the begging bowl and adopted the garb of a Sunnyasi. Since India is a place where one can do as he pleases, Purun Dass's extraordinary move was not seen as strange. Purun Dass started a life as a Sunnyasi and, wandering, depended on his neighbours for his daily bread. He never went hungry because in India neither a priest nor a beggar starves as long as there is a morsel of food to divide. Soon, Purun Dass had disappeared amongst the roving, gathering, separating millions of India.

He started calling himself Purun Bhagat and all Earth, people and food became one to him. Unconsciously, he moved towards North. He travelled through Rohtak, Karnool, Samanah and upstream along the Gugger river till he saw the great Himalayas.

"This is where I shall sit down and get knowledge," he decided and walked along the road that lead to Simla.

His journey was only just beginning. He travelled along the Himalaya — Tibet road and met many Tibetan and Indian people on the way and crossed several high passes. One day, he crossed the highest pass he had encountered till then — it had been a two-day climb — and came out on a line of snow-peaks that circled the horizon. The high mountains looked like they were close enough to hit with a stone, despite being 50 to 60 miles away. The pass was covered with dense forests of deodar and Himalayan cedar; and under the deodars stood a deserted temple of Kali — who is Durga, and also Sitala, who is worshipped against the smallpox. Purun Dass swept the floor and settled to rest.

Immediately below where he rested the hillside fell away, clean and cleared for 1500 feet, where a little village rested, with stonewalled houses and roofs of beaten earth. All around the village tiny terraced fields lay out like patchwork and cows that looked no larger than beetles grazed the smooth stone circles of the threshing-floors. One could be easily deceived by the size of things there and across the valley, the green belt that looked like low scrub was actually a forest of 100 foot pines. Purun Bhagat saw an eagle swoop across the valley and clouds which clung to the mountains, rising and then dying. "I shall find peace here," said Purun Bhagat.

As soon as the hill-men saw smoke rising from the deserted shrine, the village priest went up to welcome the stranger. As soon as he saw Purun Bhagat's eyes—the eyes that used to command thousands—he didn't say anything. He bowed low, took the begging bowl and went back to the village to tell them that they had a holy man at last. "Never have I seen such a man—a Brahmin of the Brahmins."

"Do you think he will stay?" asked the housewives and they all tried to prepare the most savoury meal out of the simple hill food that they ate.

When the priest went back with the food, he asked Purun Bhagat if he would stay, if he would need a disciple and if the food was good. Purun Bhagat ate, thanked the giver and said that he intended to stay. That was sufficient, said the priest. The village was honoured that someone like Purun Bhagat had chosen to stay with them and asked him to place the begging bowl between the two twisted roots and he would be fed daily.

That day, Purun Bhagat's wanderings ended. He was where he was meant to be, and in the silence of the space, time seemed to stop for him. He repeated a Name hundreds of times and felt himself merge with his environment increasingly.

Every morning, his begging bowl would be filled silently. Different people from the village

would have the honour of delivering the food to Purun, all anxious to get merit. Purun Bhagat watched the village from his height, for it was the only flat surface in that beautiful unnamed valley and thought of them all and wondered where it all led to at the long last.

The animals of the forest knew Kali's shrine well and soon they came to inspect who the intruder was. The *langurs*, alive with curiosity came first and after having upset the begging bowl and played around with it, decided that he was quite harmless. They came to warm themselves by the fire that Purun built and often, he would find himself sharing his blanket with a furry companion.

After the monkeys came the Barasingh, the big Deer. Once he had made friends with the solitary man, he brought his doe and fawn. At last, the smallest of the deerlets, Mushick Nabha came too, to find out what the light at the shrine meant.

Purun Bhagat would call them all "Bhai!" and draw them out if they were hiding, within earshot, in the forest. Sona, the Himalayan Bear and Purun Bhagat became best friends. The villagers saw Purun Bhagat living in harmony with the wild animals of the forest and their belief in Purun Bhagat being a miracle worker remained firm. But Purun himself aimed at performing no miracles, he simply believed that everything was one big Miracle and he strove to find his way back into the heart of things, back to the place from where his soul had come.

And so, time passed and his untrimmed hair slowly fell below his shoulders and the animals knew Purun Bhagat as their own. The village hardly changed. The priest was older, and the children who came to deliver Purun Bhagat his food, now sent their own children. If anyone asked how long the holy man had lived in the Kali's shrine, they answered, "Always."

Then came such summer rains as had not been known in the hills in many years. Purun Bhagat's shrine stood above the clouds, but for three months all he heard was the sound of tiny rivers. There was a whole month when he did not catch sight of the village at all. Then the rains relented for a week and then gathered again for one final burst of downpour. Purun Bhagat built a big fire that night, sure that his brothers would need the warmth, but none of them came.

In the middle of the night he was woken up by a faint nibbling at his blanket. A langur pulled at his hand, hard, and would not be pacified even when he was given food. Barasingh came then and pushed him towards the exit. It is then that Purun Bhagat saw that the mountain was about to fall in a gigantic landslide. He decided to not go anywhere, but then his eyes fell on the begging bowl.

"They have given me food daily since I came and I must warn them, otherwise there will not be a single mouth in the valley tomorrow. He looked at Barasingh and said, "You came to warn me, but we shall do better than that. Lend me your neck brother, for I only have two feet. He then made his way down to the village, once more Purun Dass, used to giving commands. As soon as he cleared the forest, other animals joined them.

As they reached the village, Purun Bhagat beat his crutch on the blacksmith's door and commanded them to follow. "Across the valley and up the next hill!" he shouted. Leave none behind! We follow!"

Then the people ran as only the hill people could run, because they knew that in the occasion of a landslip one must climb the highest ground across the valley. They ran up calling each other's names, the roll call of the village, and at their heels followed Barasingh, weighted down by the failing strength of Purun Bhagat. At last, the deer stopped 500 feet up the

hill side, his animal instincts telling him that he would be safe there.

Purun Bhagat stopped fainting by his side, for the cold rain and the fierce climb were killing him, but he first called to the villagers and asked them to count their numbers. He then whispered to the deer, "Stay with me, Brother. Stay — till — I — go!"

There was a sigh in the air which soon became a mutter, and then a roar, which then passed all sense of hearing. The hillside, the villagers stood on, was hit by in the darkness and rocked to the blow. The roar died away and the sound of the rain falling on miles of hard ground changed to the muffled drum of water falling on soft earth. That told its own tale. None of the villagers was bold enough to talk to the Bhagat who had saved their lives.

They waited in silence for the day and when it came they looked across the valley and saw that what had been forest and terraced field

was now one raw, red, fan-shaped smear. Of the village, the path leading up to the shrine and the shrine itself, there was no trace. For 1 mile in width and 2000 feet in sheer depth the mountain side had come away bodily, planed from head to heel.

The villagers crept through the wood to pray to their Bhagat. They saw Barasingh standing over him, who fled away when they came close. Then the langurs started wailing in the branches and Sona moaned up the hill; but their Bhagat was dead.

The priest said, "This is how all Sunnyasis must go. We will build a temple for our holy man where he rests now."

Before the year was up, they had built a small stone-and-earth shrine, and they called the hill the Bhagat's hill. They do not know that the saint they worship is the late Sir Purun Dass, once Prime Minister of the progressive and enlightened State of Mohiniwala, and honorary

or corresponding member of more learned and scientific societies that will ever do any good to this world or the next.

Chapter Three

Letting in the Jungle

Veil them, cover them, wall them round —
　　Blossom, and creeper, and weed —
Let us forget the sight and the sound,
　　The smell and the touch of the breed!
Fat black ash by the altar-stone,
　　Here is the white-foot rain,
And the does bring forth in the fields unsown,
　　And none shall affright them again;
And the blind walls crumble, unknown, o'erthrown,
　　And none shall inhabit again!

After Mowgli had pinned Shere Khan's hide
to the Council Rock, he told the remainder of the
Seeonee Pack that from then he would hunt in

the Jungle alone; and the four children of Mother and Father Wolf had said that they would hunt with him. But it is not easy to change one's life in a minute in a Jungle. Mowgli first slept for a day and a night and then told Mother Wolf and Father Wolf as much as he could of his adventures among men. Then Akela and Grey Brother explained their part in the struggle. Baloo toiled up the hill to hear all about it and Bagheera scratched himself with delight at how Mowgli had managed his war. It was long after sunrise but none of them even thought of going to sleep.

"Without Akela and Grey Brother," said Mowgli, at the end, "I could have done nothing. Oh, Mother! If only you had seen the black herd-bulls pour down the ravine, or hurry through the gates when the Man-Pack flung stones at me!"

"I am glad I did not see that last," said Mother Wolf. I don't let my cubs be driven back and forth like jackals. I would have made the

Man-Pack pay, but spared the woman who gave you milk."

"Peace, Raksha!" said father Wolf, lazily. "Our Frog has come back to us, so wise that even I must lick his feet. Leave Men alone."

"Leave Men alone," Baloo and Bagheera echoed.

Mowgli smiled, resting his head on Mother Wolf's side. He never wished to see, hear or smell Man again.

"But what if men do not leave you alone, Little Brother?" asked Akela.

"We are five," said Grey Brother, snapping his jaws.

"We also might join the hunt," said Bagheera looking at Baloo, "but why do you think of men now, Akela?"

"Because," said Akela, "I went back to the village to hide our trail, and while I did it well, Mang, the Bat, told me that Men are going around carrying guns. I have good cause to believe, "said

Akela, looking at the old scars in his flank and side, "that men do not carry guns for pleasure."

"But why should he be on our trail? Men have cast me out. What more do they need?" asked Mowgli angrily.

"You are a man, Little Brother," replied Akela. "It is not for us, the Free Hunters, to tell you what your kind do, or why."

Mowgli struck Akela's foot with a knife, but Akela's wolf instincts worked much faster. "Another time," said Mowgli quietly, "speak of the Man-Pack and of Mowgli, in two different breaths."

"That was slow," said Akela. "I could have killed a buck while you were striking."

Just then, Bagheera sat up sniffing and stiffened in every curve of his body. All the wolves followed his example.

"Man!" Akela growled.

"Buldeo follows our trails, and there is the sunlight on his gun!" said Mowgli.

"I knew that Man would follow!" cried Akela triumphantly.

"Wait!" cried Mowgli. "We must not kill any Man."

"Mowgli is right," said Bagheera. Men hunt in packs and to kill one without knowing what the rest will do is bad hunting. Come, let's see what this man wants from us."

"Look at me!" said Mowgli fiercely, as they looked at him uneasily. "Of us five, who is the leader here?"

"You are the leader, Little Brother," said grey brother, licking Mowgli's foot.

"Follow me, then," said Mowgli.

"This is what comes of living with the Man-Pack," said Bagheera, slipping down after them. "There is more in the Jungle now than Jungle Law, Baloo."

They surrounded Buldeo quietly, as only wolves can, and Mowgli translated what he heard. They had sent Buldeo to the forest to

kill the devil-child because he was the best hunter in Seeonee. In the meantime, they had captured Messua and her husband because they were clearly the parents of the Devil-child. They were to be kept prisoners till the Jungle Boy was killed. After that they would get rid of Messua and her husband as well and divide their buffaloes and lands among themselves. The English would be told that they had died of snakebite.

"Does Man trap Man?" asked Bagheera.

"So they say," replied Mowgli. "I do not understand this talk. Why must Messua and her man be put in a trap for being kind to me? I must go to the village immediately."

"And those?" asked Grey Brother.

"Sing them home," replied Mowgli with a grin. "I do not want them in the village till dark. Can you hold them?"

"Like tethered goats," replied Grey Brother with contempt.

"Go with him, Bagheera, and help him make the song and when night falls meet me at the village," said Mowgli.

"Me to sing to naked men! But let us try," said Bagheera, his eyes glittering with amusement. He lowered his head to the ground so that the sound would travel and sang a long, long midnight call of "Good Hunting." Grey Brother added to the sound with a howl that was answered by other wolves, so that the entire pack was singing along. The rough rendering of the song breaking in the afternoon hush of the jungle was this:

One moment past our bodies cast
  No shadow on the plain;
Now clear and black they stride our track,
  And we run home again.
  In morning-hush, each rock and bush
  Stands hard, and high, and raw:
Then give the Call: *"Good rest to all*
  That keep the Jungle Law!"

Now horn and pelt our peoples melt
  In covert to abide;
Now, crouched and still, to cave and hill
  Our Jungle Barons glide.
Now, stark and plain, Man's oxen strain,
  That draw the new-yoked plough;
Now, stripped and dread, the dawn is red
  Above the lit *talao*.

Ho! Get to lair! The sun's aflare
  Behind the breathing grass:
And creaking through the young bamboo
  The warning whispers pass.
By day made strange, the woods we range
  With blinking eyes we scan;
While down the skies the wild duck cries:
  "The Day – the Day to Man!"

The dew is dried that drenched our hide
  Or washed about our way;
And where we drank, the puddled bank
  Is crisping into clay.
The traitor Dark gives up each mark
  Of stretched or hooded claw;
Then hear the Call: *"Good rest to all
  That keep the Jungle Law!"*

Buldeo started repeating songs and incantations, and then went to sleep so that he could work well. Meanwhile, Mowgli rushed towards the village. It was twilight before he saw the familiar sight of the village. He was angry at mankind and yet his heart jumped to his throat when he saw that instead of getting to their usual cooking, the villagers had all gathered under a tree and there they chattered and shouted.

Mowgli crept along the outer walls till he reached Messua's house. There lay Messua, bound and gagged. She was breathing hard and groaning. Her husband was tied to the bedstead. Four men sat guarding the door that opened on the street, with their backs to the door. He crept in through the window and cut the ropes and pulled out the gags. Messua had been stoned and beaten all day long and Mowgli had to put his hand over her mouth to stop her from screaming.

"I knew he would come! Now I know for sure that he is my son!" cried Messua. Up until then Mowgli had been calm. But as he heard Messua's words, he began to tremble all over.

"Why are all these thongs? Why have they tied you?" cried Mowgli.

"For making a son out of you, why else?" said the man sullenly. "Look, I'm bleeding."

Mowgli saw Messua's wounds and the blood and gritted his teeth. "Who is responsible for this? There is price to pay."

"All the village responsible. I was too rich and had too many cattle. That is why she and I are now witches," said the man.

"I do not understand. Let Messua tell the tale," said Mowgli.

"I gave you milk, Nathoo. Do you remember?" asked Messua timidly. "Because you were my son, whom the tiger took, and because I loved you very dearly. They said that I am your mother, the mother of a devil, and therefore worthy of death."

"And what is a devil? Death I have seen," said Mowgli.

Messua laughed and said to her husband, "I knew he is no sorcerer. He is my son!"

"Your hands and feet are free now. That is the road to the Jungle. Now go!" instructed Mowgli.

"We do not know the Jungle as you do, son," said Messua. "I do not think we can walk far."

Mowgli caresses his skinning knife and said, "I have no wish to harm them — *yet*. But I do not think they will stop you. There will be a lot else to think about soon. Ah!," he lifted his head as he heard the sudden noise of shouting outside. "They have let Buldeo come home at last. Think upon where you want to go and tell me when I return." Saying so Mowgli bounded off to hear what was being said. All they did was chatter. Mowgli soon felt bored and returned to Messua's hut. At the window, he felt a touch on his foot, that he knew well.

"Mother, what are you doing here?" asked Mowgli.

"I heard my children singing in the woods and followed the one I love best. Little Frog, I want to see the woman who gave you milk."

"They had bound her and meant to kill her. I have freed them and she is going towards the Jungle with her man."

"I will follow, for I am not yet toothless," said Mother Wolf. "I gave you first milk, but Bagheera is right. Man always returns to man at the last."

"Maybe," replied Mowgli with an unpleasant look on his face, "but I am far from that trail tonight. Wait here so that they do not see you."

"*You* were never afraid of *me*, Little Frog," said Mother Wolf as she faded into the bushes, as she knew how.

"So," said Mowgli cheerfully as he swung back into the house, "they are all sitting around

Baldeo, who is telling them that which didn't happen. They will come when he has finished talking. Then?"

"I have talked to my man," replied Messua. "Thirty miles from here is Khanhiwara. All white people live there. They govern over all lands and do not let anyone be punished without witnesses. If we can get there, we will live, otherwise, we will die."

"Live, then," said Mowgli. "No one else shall cross the village gates tonight. But what does he do." he asked gesturing to the man frantically gigging up the floor.

"It is a little money to buy a horse with. We cannot walk so far."

"You know the trail to Khanhiwara?" Mowgli asked Messua. When she nodded, he continued, "Go, then. Not a tooth in the Jungle is bared against you, nor a foot lifted against you. You will hear the Jungle sing, but do not be afraid. It is Favour of the Jungle. You shall have protective eyes on you tell you are within earshot of Khanhiwara.

As they walked away, Mother Wolf sprang out of the tall grass, called out to Bagheera and then followed Messua and her husband.

Bagheera came to Mowgli and said, "Let me deal with the Man-Pack alone. I am Bagheera and the strength of the night is in me. With one strike of my paw I can beat your head as flat as a dead frog!"

"Strike then," said Mowgli in the dialect of the village. The words said in man's tongue brought Bagheera to a full stop. He quivered with his head level with Mowgli's. Mowgli stared back rebelliously, until Bagheera's head lowered and he licked Mowgli's foot. Mowgli stoked Bagheera's head lightly and steadily. "Brother! Be Still! It is the fault of the night and not yours."

They stayed that way for some time, Bagheera recovering from the overpowering smells of the village.

"You are of the Jungle and *not* of the Jungle. And I am only a black Panther. But I love you, Little Brother."

Mowgli chose not to notice the last line and said that Baldeo and the villagers must be coming to get Messua and her husband soon. Instead they should arrange for a trap.

"No! Listen. Let them find me instead. They will not try to put me in chains I think."

"Be it so," said Mowgli.

Soon the villagers came and after struggling with the firmly fastened lock, they entered the hut. There sat Bagheera on the bed. There was half a minute of desperate silence from the villagers, in which time Bagheera raised his head and yawned—elaborately, carefully and ostentatiously—as he would yawn to insult an equal. Then the lips curls, the red tongue rolled out and the jaw dropped till one could see halfway down the dark gullet. His teeth stuck out. The next moment the streets

were empty, all hurrying to get to their huts as quickly as possible.

"They will not come out till daybreak," said Bagheera, joining Mowgli again.

He was right. They did not steer for the rest of the night, but Mowgli's face grew darker and darker. He slept through the day and when he woke up at night Bagheera was at his side and informed him that Messua and her man had reached Khanhiwara quite quickly and safely.

"There is nothing more to do. Forget the Man-Pack and come hunting with me and Baloo." said Bagheera.

"They will be forgotten soon," said Mowgli, "but where is Hathi tonight?"

"Where he chooses to be. Who can tell about the Silent One?," replied Bagheera.

"Tell him and his sons to see me," said Mowgli.

"But they are not to say Come or Go to Hathi. Remember, he taught you the Master-words of the forest.'

"That is all ok," replied Mowgli." I have a master word for him now. Tell him to come because of the Sack of the fields of Bhurtpore.

Much to Bagheera's surprise, Mowgli's words proved true. They came, obedient to the call.

"I know what happened in Bhurtpore," said Mowgli.

Thus prompted, Hathi recounted how he had been captured in a trap and badly injured by a man-tribe in Bhurtpore. He had managed to escape, but he had been in a rage of pain, which had led him to completely destroy five villages. "I let in the Jungle in five villages."

"I have seen the blood of the woman who was kind to me and gave me food. They would kill from their own tribe. They cannot stay here," declared Mowgli, shaking with anger. "I want you to let in the Jungle in the village."

"But it requires great anger, fear and pain to destroy so many lives. I cannot do it now," replied Hathi, fearfully.

"There are other ways to let in the Jungle. Ask everyone to help. Let them take over the village. Let the villagers know that they can find no food here," said Mowgli.

Bagheera saw the cunning plan that would force the villagers to desert their lands and was awed. "Are you the same naked thing that I defended when all was young? Mowgli, you are a Master, and you must speak for me when I am old and weak."

The idea of Bagheera old and week upset Mowgli and he distracted himself. In the meantime, Hathi made his slow progress towards the village. Somewhere in the Jungle a rumour started that there was good food to be found near the village and all kinds of Jungle people moved towards the location to explore their options. In 10 days, there were all kinds of grass eaters who had started living around the village fields. The flesh-eaters, following close behind, pushed them even closer to the village.

When Hathi arrived with his sons, it was the dead of the night. They started breaking off the poles of the *machans* that the villagers used to sit on. The noise and the commotion that followed led to the animals assembled in near the fields to scurry in all directions. The sharp hooves of the animals destroyed the young and delicate crops.

When the villagers woke up the next morning, they saw that all their crops were destroyed and that they must go elsewhere or starve. Slowly, over the months, their food stores declined. They still stayed, but then the rains came and they realised that there was no way other than asking the white people in Khanhiwara for help. After they left, Hathi and his sons demolished what was left of the buildings in the village. A month later, green mould dimpled the deserted village and then, there was the roaring Jungle in the spot which had been ploughed by men barely six months ago.

Mowgli's Song Against People

I will let loose against you the fleet-footed vines —
I will call in the Jungle to stamp out your lines!
The roofs shall fade before it,
The house-beams shall fall;
And the *Karela*, the bitter *Karela*,
Shall cover it all!
In the gates of these your councils my people shall sing.
In the doors of these your garners the Bat-folk shall cling;
And the snake shall be your watchman,
By a hearthstone unswept;
For the *Karela*, the bitter *Karela*,
Shall fruit where ye slept!
Ye shall not see my strikers; ye shall hear them and guess.
By night, before the moon-rise, I will send for my cess,
And the wolf shall be your herdsman
By a landmark removed;
For the Karela, the bitter Karela,
Shall seed where ye loved!
I will reap your fields before you at the hands of a host.
Ye shall glean behind my reapers for the bread that is lost;
And the deer shall be your oxen
On a headland untilled;
For the Karela, the bitter Karela,

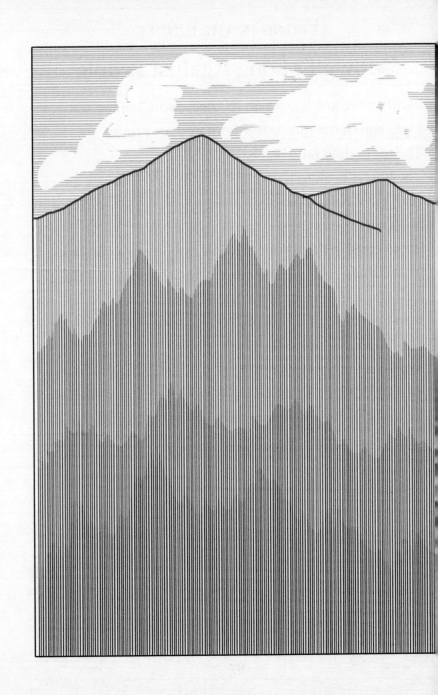

Shall leaf where ye build !

I have untied against you the club-footed vines —

I have sent in the Jungle to swamp out your lines!

The trees — the trees are on you!

The house-beams shall fall;

And the Karela, the bitter Karela,

Shall cover you all !

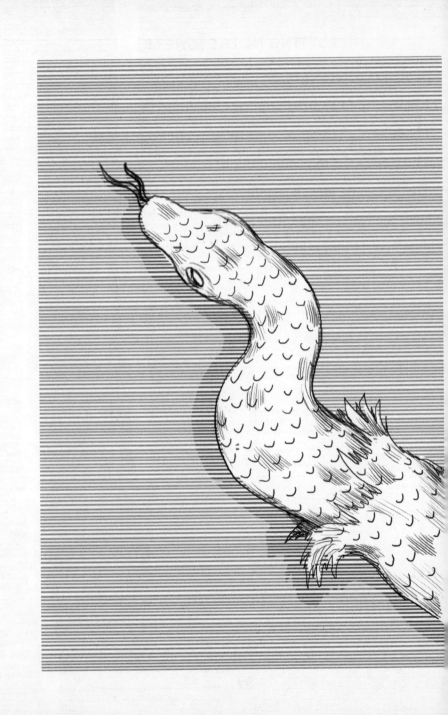

Chapter 4

The King's Ankus

Kaa, the big Rock Python, had changed his skin for the 200th time since his birth. Mowgli never forgot that he owed his life to Kaa and he was with Kaa, this time. Skin-changing always makes a snake moody and depressed until the new skin begins to shine and look beautiful. Kaa never made fun of Mowgli anymore and Kaa accepted Mowgli as the Master of the Jungle as all the other Jungle People did. He brought Mowgli all the news of all the Jungle a Python his size would naturally hear.

What Kaa didn't know about the Middle Jungle — the life that runs close to the earth or

101

under it, the boulder, burrow and the tree-bole life—might have been written on the smallest of Kaa's scales.

This afternoon Mowgli was sitting in the circle of Kaa's great coils, fingering the flaked and broken old skin that looped and twisted among the rocks just as Kaa had left it. Kaa had very courteously packed himself under Mowgli's broad, bare shoulders, so that the boy was in effect resting on a living armchair.

"It is perfect even to the scales of the eyes," said Mowgli. "It must be strange to see one's own head at one's feet."

"Yes, but I have no feet," said Kaa. "And since it is a custom with our people I do not find it strange. Does your skin never feel old and harsh?"

"Then I go and wash," retorted Mowgli. "But you are right, when it gets hot, I have wished that I could shed my skin and run skinless."

"I wash and shed my skin. How does my new skin look?"

Mowgli ran his fingers down the diagonal chequering of the immense back. "The turtle is harder-backed but not so bright, the frog is brighter but not so hard. It is very beautiful to see."

"It needs water. A new skin never comes to full colour before the first bath. Let us go, bathe."

"I will carry you," said Mowgli; and he stooped down, laughing, to lift the middle section of Kaa's great body, just where the barrel was thickest. Kaa lay still, puffing with quiet amusement. Then the regular evening game began—the Boy in the flush of his great strength, and the Python in his luxurious new skin, standing up one against the other for a wrestling match—a trial of eye and strength. Of course, Kaa could have crushed a dozen Mowglis if he had let himself go, but he played carefully, and never let loose one-tenth of his power. Ever since Mowgli was strong enough to endure a little rough handling, Kaa had taught him this game, and it strengthened his limbs as nothing else could. Sometimes Mowgli would stand lapped almost to his throat in Kaa's shifting coils, striving to get one arm free and catch him by the throat. Then Kaa would give way limply, and Mowgli, with both quick-moving feet would try to cramp the purchase of that huge tail as it flung backward feeling for a rock or a stump.

The game always ended in one way — with a straight, driving blow of the head that knocked the boy over and over. Mowgli could never learn the guard for that lightning lunge and, as Kaa said, there was no use in trying.

"Good hunting!" Kaa grunted at last. Mowgli, as usual, was shot away half a dozen yards, gasping and laughing. He rose with his fingers full of grass, and followed Kaa to the wise snake's pet bathing-place — a deep, pitchy-

black pool surrounded with rocks, and made interesting by sunken tree-stumps. The boy slipped in, in Jungle-fashion, without a sound, and dived across; rose, too, without a sound, and turned on his back, his arms behind his head, watching the moon rising above the rocks, and breaking up her reflection in the water with his toes. Kaa's diamond-shaped head cut the pool like a razor, and came out to rest on Mowgli's shoulder. They lay still, soaking luxuriously in the cool water.

"It is *very* good," said Mowgli at last, sleepily.

"Now, in the Man-Pack, at this hour, as I remember, they laid them down upon hard pieces of wood in the inside of a mud-trap, and, having carefully shut out all the clean winds, drew foul cloth over their heavy heads and made evil songs through their noses. It is better in the Jungle."

A hurrying cobra slipped down over a rock and drank, said "Good hunting!" and went away.

"Sssh!," said Kaa, as though he had suddenly remembered something.

"So, the Jungle gives you all that you have ever wanted, Little Brother?"

"Not all," said Mowgli, laughing, "otherwise there would be a new and strong Shere Khan to kill once a month. I could kill with my own hands, asking no help of buffaloes. And, I have wished the sun to shine in the middle of the Rains, and the Rains to cover the sun in the summer. I have always wished that my kill was bigger."

"You have no other desire? ' the big snake demanded.

"What more can I wish for? I have the Jungle! Is there more anywhere between sunrise and sunset?"

"Now, the Cobra said –," Kaa began.

"What cobra?"

"He that went away just now said nothing. He was hunting."

"It was another."

"Do you often talk to the poison people? I give them their own path. They carry death in the fore-tooth, and that is not good—for they are so small. But which snake have you spoken with?" Kaa rolled slowly in the water like a steamer in a beam sea.

"Three or four months ago," said he, "I hunted in Cold Lairs. And the thing I hunted ran shrieking past the tanks and to that house whose side I once broke for your sake, and ran into the ground."

"But the people of Cold Lairs do not live in burrows." Mowgli knew that Kaa was telling of the Monkey People.

This thing was not living, but seeking to live," Kaa replied, with a quiver of his tongue.

"He ran into a burrow that led very far. I followed, and having killed, I slept. When I woke up, I went forward."

"Under the earth?"

"Yes, coming at last upon a White Cobra, who spoke of things beyond my knowledge, and showed me many things I had never seen."

"New game? Was it good hunting?" Mowgli turned quickly on his side.

"It was no game, and would have broken all my teeth, but the White Cobra said that a man would die for only the sight of those things."

"We will look," said Mowgli. "I now remember that I was once a man."

"Slowly — slowly. A yellow snake who swallowed the Sun died because of hurry. We two spoke together under the earth, and I spoke of you, naming you as a man.

Said the White Hood (and he is indeed as old as the Jungle), "It is long since I have seen a man, Let him come, and he shall see all these things, for the least of which very many men would die." "That *must* be new game. And yet the Poison People do not tell us when game is afoot. They are an unfriendly folk."

"It is *not* game. It is — it is — I cannot say what it is."

"We will go there. I have never seen a White Hood, and I wish to see the other things. Did he kill them?"

'They are all dead things. He says he is the keeper of them all."

"Ah! As a wolf stands above meat he has taken to his own lair. Let us go."

Mowgli swam to bank, rolled on the grass to dry himself, and the two set off for Cold Lairs, the deserted city.

Mowgli was not the least afraid of the Monkey People in those days, but the Monkey People had the liveliest horror of Mowgli. Their tribes, however, were raiding in the Jungle, and so Cold Lairs stood empty and silent in the moonlight. Kaa led up to the ruins of the queens' pavilion that stood on the terrace, slipped over the rubbish, and dived down the half-choked staircase that went underground from the centre of the pavilion. Kaa gave the White Cobra a call and went in. Mowgli followed on his hands and knees. They crawled over a long distance down a sloping passage that turned and twisted several times, and at last came to where the root of some great tree, growing 30 feet overhead, had forced out a solid stone in the wall. They crept through the gap, and found themselves in a large, dark vault. "A safe lair," said Mowgli, rising to his feet, "but too far to visit daily. And now what do we see?"

"Am I nothing?" said a voice in the dark, and Mowgli saw something white move until the largest Cobra Mowgli had ever seen emerged before him. Even the spectacle-marks of his spread hood had faded to faint yellow. His eyes were as red as rubies, and altogether he was most wonderful.

"Good hunting!" said Mowgli, who carried his manners with his knife, and that never left him.

"What of the city?" said the White Cobra, without answering *the* greeting. "What *of the* great, the walled city — the city of a 100 elephants and 20,000 horses, and cattle past counting — the city of the King of Twenty Kings? I grow deaf here, and it is long since I heard their war-gongs."

"The Jungle is above our heads," said Mowgli. "I know only Hathi and his sons among elephants. Bagheera has slain all the horses in one village, and — what is a King?"

"I told you," said Kaa softly to the Cobra, "I told you three months ago that there is no city here."

"The city — the great city of the forest whose gates are guarded by the King's towers — can never pass. They built it before my father's father came from the egg, and it shall endure when my son's sons are as white as Salomdhi, son of Chandrabija, son of Viyeja, son of Yegasuri, made it in the days of Bappa Rawal. Whose cattle are you?"

"It is a lost trail," said Mowgli, turning to Kaa. "I do not know his talk."

"Nor I. He is very old. Father of Cobras, there is only the Jungle here, as it has been since the beginning."

"Then who is *he*," said the White Cobra, "sitting down before me, unafraid, knowing not the name of the King, talking our talk through a man's lips? Who is he with the knife and the snake's tongue."

"They call me Mowgli," was the answer. "I am of the Jungle. The wolves are my people, and Kaa here is my brother. Father of Cobras, who are you?"

"I am the Warden of the King's Treasure. Kurrun Raja built the stone above me, in the days when my skin was dark, so that I could kill those who came to steal. Then they let down the treasure through the stone. Five times since I came here has the stone been lifted, but always to let down more, and never to take away. There are no riches like these riches—the treasures of a hundred kings. But it has been a long time since the stone was last moved, and I think that my city has forgotten."

"There is no city. Look up. There are roots of the great trees tearing the stones apart. Trees and men do not grow together," Kaa insisted.

"Twice and thrice have men found their way here," the White Cobra answered savagely, "but they never spoke till I came upon them groping in the dark, and then they cried only a little. But *you* come with lies, Man and Snake both, and would have me believe the city is gone, and that my guardianship has ended. Until the stone is lifted, and the Brahmins come down singing the songs that I know, and feed me with warm milk, and take me to the light again, only I am the Warden of the King's Treasure. The city is dead, you say, and here are the roots of the trees? Take what you will, then. Earth has no treasure like to these. Man with the snake's tongue, if you can go alive by the way that you have entered, the lesser King's will be your servants."

"Again, the trail is lost," said Mowgli coolly.

"Can any jackal have burrowed so deep and bitten this great White Hood. He is surely mad. Father of Cobras, I see nothing here to take away."

"Madness of death upon the boy!" hissed the Cobra.

"Before your eyes close I will allow you this favour. Look and see what no other man has never seen before."

"They do not do well in the Jungle who speak to Mowgli of favours," said the boy, "but the dark changes all, as I know. But I will look."

He stared with puckered-up eyes round the vault, and then lifted from the floor a handful of something that glittered.

"Oho! this is like the stuff they play with in the Man-Pack: only this is yellow and the other was brown."

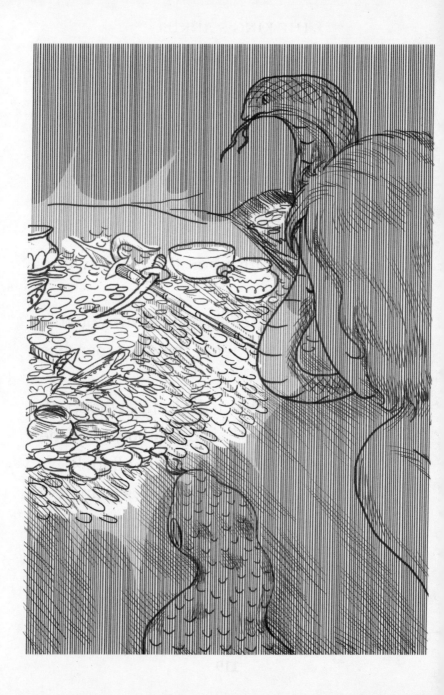

He let the gold pieces fall, and moved forward. The floor of the vault was buried some five or six feet deep in coined gold and silver that had burst from the sacks it had been originally stored in, and, in the long years, the metal had packed and settled as sand packs at low tide. On it and in it, and rising through it, as wrecks lift through the sand, were jewelled elephant-howdahs of embossed silver, studded with plates of hammered gold, and adorned with carbuncles and turquoises.

The White Cobra was right. No money would begin to pay the value of this treasure, the sifted pickings of centuries of war, plunder, trade and taxation. The coins alone were priceless, leaving out of count all the precious stones; and the dead weight of the gold and silver alone might be two or three hundred tons. Every native ruler in India today, however poor, has a hoard to which he is always adding and keeps the knowledge of it very closely to themselves. But Mowgli naturally did not understand what these things meant. The knives interested him a little, but they did not balance so well as his own, and so he dropped them. At last he found something fascinating half buried in the coins. It was a three-foot ankus, or elephant-goad—something like a small boat hook. The top was one round, shining ruby, and eight inches of the handle below it were studded with rough turquoises close together, giving a most satisfactory grip. Below them was a rim of jade with a flower-pattern running around it—only the leaves were emeralds, and the blossoms were rubies sunk in the cool, green stone. The rest of the handle was a shaft of pure ivory, while the point—the spike and hook—was gold-inlaid steel with pictures of elephant-catching; and the pictures attracted Mowgli, who saw that they had something to do with his friend Hathi the Silent.

The White Cobra had been following him closely, "Is seeing this not worth dying?" he said. "Have I not done you a great favour?"

"I do not understand," said Mowgli. "The things are hard and cold, and by no means good to eat. But this" — he lifted the ankus — "I want to take away, that I may see it in the sun. These are all yours? Will you give it to me? I will bring you frogs to eat."

The White Cobra fairly shook with evil delight.

"Of course, I will give it," he said. "All that is here I will give you — till you go away."

"But I am going now. This place is dark and cold, and I wish to take the thorn-pointed thing to the Jungle."

"Look by your foot! What is that there?"

Mowgli picked up something that was that was white and smooth.

"It is the bone of a man's head," he said quietly. "And here are two more."

"I spoke *to* them in the dark, and they lay still."

"But what do I need of this that is called treasure? If you will give me the ankus to

take away, it is good hunting. If not, it is good hunting none the less. I do not fight with the Poison People, and I was also taught the Master-word *of* your tribe."

"There is but one Master-word here. It is mine," Kaa flung himself forward with blazing eyes.

"Who told me to bring the Man?" he hissed.

"I did," the old Cobra lisped. "It has been long since I have seen a Man, and this Man speaks our tongue."

"But there was no talk of killing. How can I go to the Jungle and say that I have led him to his death?" said Kaa.

"I do not talk of killing till the time comes. And as to your going or not going, there is the hole in the wall. Never did Man come here and go away alive. I am the Warden of the Treasure of the King's City."

"But there is no city! The forest is all about us!" cried Kaa.

"The Treasure is still here. Wait awhile, Kaa of the Rocks, and see the boy run. There is chance for great sport here. Life is good. Run to and fro for a while, and make a sport, boy!"

Mowgli put his hand on Kaa's head quietly. "The white thing has dealt with men of the Man-Pack until now. He does not know me," he whispered. "He has asked for his hunting. Let him have it." Mowgli had been standing with the ankus held point down. He flung it from him quickly and it dropped crossways just behind the great snake's hood, pinning him to the floor. In a flash, Kaa's weight was upon the writhing body, paralysing it from hood to tail. The red eyes burned, and the six spare inches of the head struck furiously right and left.

"I will never kill again save for food. But look Kaa!" He caught the snake behind the hood, forced the mouth open with the blade of the knife, and showed the terrible poison-fangs of the upper jaw lying black and withered in the gum. The White Cobra had outlived his poison, as a snake will.

"It is dried up," said Mowgli, and motioning Kaa away, he picked up the ankus, setting the White Cobra free.

"I am ashamed. You must kill me!" hissed the White Cobra.

"There has been too much talk of killing. We will go now. I take the thorn-pointed thing, because I have fought and beaten you."

"See, then, that the thing does not kill you at last. It is Death! Remember, it is Death. There is enough in that thing to kill all the men of my city. You will not hold it for long, nor will he who takes it from you, but the ankus will do my work. It is Death!"

Mowgli crawled out through the hole into the passage again, and the last that he saw was the White Cobra striking furiously with his harmless fangs on the floor, and hissing, "It is Death!"

They were glad to get to the light of day once more; and when they were back in their own Jungle and Mowgli made the ankus glitter in the morning light, he was almost as pleased as though he had found a bunch of new flowers to stick in his hair.

"This is brighter than Bagheera's eyes," he said delightedly, as he twirled the ruby. "I will show it to him, but what did he mean when he talked of death?"

"I cannot say. I am sorrowful to my tail's tail that he did not feel your knife. There is always evil at Cold Lairs—above ground or below. But now I am hungry. Will you hunt with me this morning?" asked Kaa.

"No. Bagheera must see this thing. Good hunting!" Mowgli danced off, flourishing the great ankus, and stopping from time to time to admire it, till he came to that part of the Jungle Bagheera chiefly used, and found him drinking after a heavy kill. Mowgli told him

all his adventures from beginning to end, and Bagheera sniffed at the ankus. When Mowgli came to the White Cobra's last words, the Panther purred approvingly.

"Then the White Hood spoke the thing which is?" Mowgli asked quickly.

"I was born in the King's cages at Oodeypore, and it is in my stomach that I know some little of Man, very many men would kill thrice in a night for the sake of that one big red stone alone."

"But the stone makes it heavy to the hand. My little bright knife is better. And—see! The red stone is not good to eat. Then *why* would they kill?"

"Mowgli, go and sleep. Men kill for idleness and pleasure."

"For what use was this thorn-pointed thing made?" persisted Mowgli.

Bagheera half opened his eyes—he was very sleepy—with a malicious twinkle.

"It was made by men to thrust into the head of the sons of Hathi, so that the blood should pour out. I have seen the like in the street of Oodeypore, before our cages. That thing has tasted the blood of many such as Hathi."

"But why do they thrust into the heads of elephants?"

"To teach them Man's Law. Having neither claws nor teeth, men make these things — and others that are worse."

"Always more blood when I come near, even to the things the Man-Pack have made," said Mowgli disgustedly. He was getting a little tired of the weight of the ankus. "If I had known this, I would not have taken it."

"I am going to sleep. Little Brother. I cannot hunt all night and howl all day, as do some folk."

Bagheera went off to a hunting-lair that he knew, about two miles off. Mowgli made an easy way for himself up a convenient tree, and knotted three or four creepers together. Though he had no positive objection to strong daylight, Mowgli followed the custom of his friends, and used it as little as he could.

When Mowgli woke up, it was evening and he realised that he had been dreaming about the bright stones that he had left behind. He went to the ankus and found it missing. Bagheera came up too and said a man had carried it away.

"So, we can find out if the ankus is really cursed. He should die, who has taken the ankus away."

They hunted first, because an empty stomach makes for a careless eye. They then followed the tracks of the man in the forest, clear because of the heavy weight of the ankus on the wet floor.

They followed the footprints to some distance, until it was met by another man's footprints. They followed both trails and soon found the body of a villager lying dead, an arrow through his chest.

"Here is at least one death," said Mowgli.

Once more they followed the single trail that led away. But alas, this also led them to another dead man. He lay near the ashes of a large bonfire and four tracks of footprints led away from the dead body. And they now followed the broad tracks of four footprints. Sometime later they came upon four more dead people. It was easy to inspect and see what had happened. One of them had used poison to cook food for the other three. Those three had killed the cook, and then died of eating the poisoned food.

"The ankus does its work fast," commented Bagheera.

"I should not have brought this into the forest. It has already killed six times tonight."

"It is not your fault."

"Even then, I shall not repeat this folly," said Mowgli.

Two nights later, while the White Cobra sat mourning in the darkness of the vault, ashamed,

robbed, and alone, the turquoise ankus whirled through the hole in the wall, and clashed on the floor of golden coins.

"Father of Cobras," said Mowgli (he was careful to keep the other side of the wall), "get a young one of your own people to help you guard the King's Treasure, so that no man may come away alive anymore."

"Ah-ha! It returns, then. I told you the thing was Death. How come you are still alive?" the old Cobra mumbled, twining lovingly round the ankus.

"I do not know! That thing has killed six times in a night. Let it go out no more."

Chapter 5

Red Dog

It was after the letting in of the Jungle that the pleasantest part of Mowgli's life began. All the Jungle was his friend, and just a little afraid of him. The things that he did and saw and heard when he was wandering, with or without his four companions, would make many stories, each as long as this one.

But we must tell one tale at a time. Father and Mother Wolf died, and Mowgli rolled a big boulder against the mouth of their cave, and cried the Death Song over them. Baloo grew very old and stiff, and even Bagheera, whose nerves were steel and whose muscles were iron, was a

shade slower on the kill than he had been. Akela turned from grey to milky white with pure age. His ribs stuck out, and he walked as though he had been made of wood, and Mowgli killed for him. But the young wolves, the children of the disbanded Seeonee Pack, throve and increased, and when there were about 40 of them, full-voiced, clean-footed five-year-olds, Akela told them that they ought to gather themselves together and follow the Law, and run under one head, as befitted the Free People.

This was not a question in which Mowgli concerned himself, for, as he said, he had eaten sour fruit, and he knew the tree it hung from; but when Phao, son of Phaona (his father was the Grey Tracker in the days of Akela's headship), fought his way to the leadership of the Pack, according to the Jungle Law, and the old calls and songs began to ring under the stars once more, Mowgli came to the Council Rock for memory's sake. When he chose to speak

the Pack waited till he had finished, and he sat at Akela's side on the rock above Phao. Those were days of good hunting and good sleeping. No stranger cared to break into the jungles that belonged to Mowgli's people, as they called the Pack, and the young wolves grew fat and strong, and there were many cubs to bring to the Looking-over. Mowgli always attended a Looking-over, remembering the night when a black panther brought a naked brown baby into the pack, and the long call, 'Look, look well, O Wolves,' made his heart flutter.

One twilight when he was trotting leisurely across the ranges to give Akela the half of a buck that he had killed, while the Four jogged behind him, sparring a little, and tumbling one another over for joy of being alive, he heard a cry that had never been heard since the bad days of Shere Khan. It was what they call in the Jungle the pheeal, a hideous kind of shriek that the jackal gives when he is hunting behind a tiger, or when

there is a big killing afoot. The Four stopped at once, bristling and growling. Mowgli's hand went to his knife, and he checked, the blood in his face, his eyebrows knotted.

"It is some great killing. Listen carefully!" said Grey Brother.

It broke out again, half sobbing and half chuckling, just as though the jackal had soft human lips. Then Mowgli drew deep breath, and ran to the Council Rock, overtaking on his way hurrying wolves of the Pack. Phao and Akela were on the Rock together, and below them, every nerve strained, sat the others. The mothers and the cubs were cantering off to their lairs. They could hear nothing except the Waingunga rushing and gurgling in the dark, and the light evening winds among the tree-tops, till suddenly across the river a wolf called. It was no wolf of the Pack, for they were all at the Rock.

"Dhole!" it said, "Dhole! Dhole! Dhole!" They heard tired feet on the rocks, and a gaunt

wolf, streaked with red on his flanks, his right fore-paw useless, and his jaws white with foam, flung-himself into the circle and lay gasping at Mowgli's feet. He was a solitary wolf, Wontolla, fending for himself, his mate and his cubs in some lonely lair, as do many wolves in the south. Then he panted, and they could see his heart-beats shake him backward and forward.

"The dhole, the dhole of the Dekkan—Red Dog, the Killer! They came north from the south saying the Dekkan was empty and killing out by the way. When this moon was new there were four to me—my mate and three cubs. She would teach them to kill on the grass plains, hiding to drive the buck, as we do who are of the open. At midnight I heard them together, full tongue on the trail. At the dawn-wind I found them stiff in the grass. Then I sought my Blood-Right and found the dhole."

"How many?" said Mowgli quickly.

"I do not know."

He thrust out his mangled fore-foot, all dark with dried blood. There were cruel bites low down on his side, and his throat was torn.

"Eat," said Akela, rising up from the meat Mowgli had brought him, and the Wolf flung himself on it.

"This shall be no loss," he said humbly, when he had taken off the first edge of his hunger. "Give me a little strength, Free People, and I also will kill."

"We shall need those jaws," said he. "Were there cubs with the dhole?"

"No, no. They are all grown dogs of their Pack, heavy and strong for all that they eat lizards in the Dekkan."

What Won-tolla had said meant that the dhole, the red hunting-dog of the Dekkan, was moving to kill, and the Pack knew well that even the tiger will surrender a new kill to the dhole. They drive straight through the Jungle, and what they meet they pull down and tear to pieces. Though they are not as big nor half as cunning as the wolf, they are very strong and very numerous. The dhole, for instance, do not begin to call themselves a pack till they are a hundred, whereas forty wolves make a very fair pack indeed. Mowgli's wanderings had taken him to the edge of the high grassy downs of the Dekkan, and he had seen the fearless dholes sleeping and playing and scratching themselves in the little hollows and tussocks that they use for lairs. He despised and hated them because they did not smell like the Free People, because they did not live in caves, and, above all, because they had hair between their toes while he and his friends were clean-footed. But he knew, for Hathi had told him, what a terrible thing a dhole hunting pack was. Even Hathi moves aside from their line, and until they are killed, or till game is scarce, they will go forward.

Akela said to Mowgli quietly, "It is better to die in a Full Pack than leaderless and alone.

This is good hunting, and — my last. But, as men live, you have very many more nights and days, Little Brother. Go north and lie down, and if any live after the dhole has gone by he shall bring you news of the fight. It is to the death and you have never met the dhole — the Red Killer."

"Aowa! Aowa!," said Mowgli, "I say that when the dhole come, and if the dhole come, Mowgli and the Free People are of one skin for that hunting."

"You do not know the dhole, man with a wolf's tongue," said Won-tolla.

"I look only to clear the Blood Debt against them before they kill me. They move slowly, killing out as they go, but in two days a little strength will come back to me. But you Free People, should go north and eat little for a while till the dhole are gone."

"No, we fight!," said Mowgli. "We will need every tooth and jaw for the fight. I will go count the dogs."

"It is death!" said Won-tolla, "what will a hairless one like you do against the dhole?"

"You are an outsider and do not know me. We will speak once the dogs are dead," retorted Mowgli and was on his way. He reached Kaa, in excitement.

"You make too much noise!" said Kaa angrily, as he lay keeping a keen eye on the deer trail.

"It was my fault, Kaa," said Mowgli meekly. "But every time I see you, you grow larger and thicker. There is no one like you in the Jungle, wise, old strong and beautiful."

And then he told Kaa everything that had happened.

"Wise I may be," said Kaa at the end, "but deaf I surely am. Else I should have heard the pheeal. Small wonder the Eaters of Grass are uneasy. How many are the dhole?"

"I have not yet seen. I came to you as fast as I could. You are older than Hathi. But oh, Kaa," — here Mowgli wriggled with sheer

joy — "it will be good hunting. Few of us will see another moon."

"Will you also fight in this?" asked Kaa. "Remember, the Pack has cast you out. Let the wolves look to the dogs. You are a Man."

"I am a Wolf" cried Mowgli.

"It is folly to tie yourself for the sake of the memory of dead wolves. This is not good hunting!"

"So be it. But I am of the Free People until the dhole have gone by. It is my Word and has been heard by all."

"I had thought I would carry you away to the north. But what do you have in mind now?"

"When they cross the river, I shall meet them with the pack behind me and stab them."

"If that is your plan, then there is no one that will survive. There will only remain dry bones. I have lived many years. Let me think a bit about what might be a better plan."

And so as Kaa thought, Mowgli went to sleep, resting in his great coils. When Mowgli woke up, he found Kaa ready and energised.

"Come to the river with me," he said, "do not swim, I am faster, so climb on my back."

Mowgli tucked his left arm round Kaa's neck, dropped his right close to his body, and straightened his feet. Then Kaa breasted the current as he alone could, and the ripple of the checked water stood up in a frill round Mowgli's neck, and his feet were waved to and fro in the eddy under the python's lashing sides. A mile or two above the Peace Rock, the Waingunga narrows between a gorge of marble rocks from 80–100 feet high, and the current runs like a mill-race between and over, all manner of ugly stones.

Kaa came to anchor with a double twist of his tail round a sunken rock, holding Mowgli in the hollow of a coil, while the water raced on.

"This is the place of Death," said Mowgli, for they had reached that place where the Little

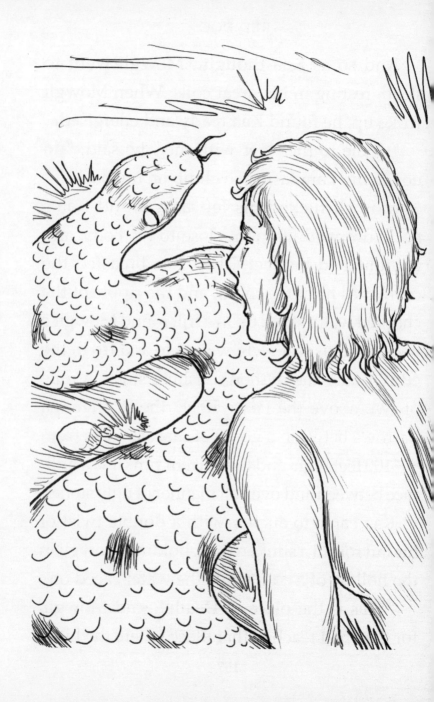

People of the Rocks lived. The hives of the wild Black Beas of India were dreaded by all. Kaa moved upstream again till he came to a sandy bar at the head of the gorge.

"Now I will tell you. A hunted buck from the south, many, many years ago, came here from the south, not knowing the Jungle, a Pack on his trail. Blinded by fear, he leaped from above. Many were those of the Pack who leaped into the Waingunga, but they were dead before they took water. Those who did not leap died also in the rocks above. But the buck lived."

"How ?"

"Because he came first, running for his life, leaping before the Little People were aware, and was in the river when they gathered to kill. The Pack, following, was altogether lost under the weight of the Little People."

"The buck lived?" Mowgli repeated slowly.

"At least he did not die then, though none waited his coming down with a strong body

to hold him safe against the water, as a certain old fat, deaf, yellow Flathead would wait for a Manling though there were all the dholes of the Dekkan on his trail. What is in your mind?" Kaa's head was close to Mowgli's ear, and it was some time before the boy answered.

"Kaa, you are, indeed, the wisest of all the Jungle."

"So many have said. Look now, if the dhole follow you..."

"I will make them follow."

"If they follow you, looking only at your shoulders, those who do not die up above will fall in the water, for the Waingunga is hungry water, and they will have no Kaa to hold them, but will go down, such as live, to the shallows by the Seeonee Lairs, and there your Pack may meet them to fight."

'Ahai! Eowawa! There is now only the little matter of the run and the leap. I will make sure that the dholes follow me very closely."

Have you seen the rocks above you?"

"Indeed, no. That I had forgotten."

"Go look. It is all rotten ground, cut and full of holes. One of your clumsy feet set down without seeing would end the hunt. I will leave you here, and for your sake only I will carry word to the Pack that they may know where to look for the dhole. For myself, I am not of one skin with any wolf."

When Kaa disliked an acquaintance he could be more unpleasant than any of the Jungle People, except perhaps Bagheera. He swam downstream, and opposite the Rock he met Phao and Akela listening to the night noises.

"Hssh! Dogs," he said cheerfully. "The dholes will come downstream. If you are not afraid you can kill them in the shallows."

"When do they come?" said Phao. "And where is my Man-cub?" said Akela.

"They will come when they come," said Kaa. "Wait and see. As for your Man-cub, from whom you have taken a Word and so laid him open to Death, your Man-cub is with me and if he is not already dead it is no thanks to you, bleached dog! Wait here for the dhole, and be glad that the Man-cub and I strike on your side."

Kaa flashed upstream again, and moored himself in the middle of the gorge, looking upward at the line of the cliff. Presently he saw Mowgli's head move against the stars, and then there was a whizz in the air, the keen, clean schloop of a body falling feet first, and next minute the boy was at rest again in the loop of Kaa's body.

"It is certainly no leap to make at night," said Mowgli quietly.

"I have jumped twice as far for fun, but that is an evil place above—low bushes and gullies that go down very deep, all full of the Little People. I have put big stones one above the other by the side of three gullies. These I shall throw down with my feet in running, and the Little People will rise up behind me, very angry."

"That is Man's talk and Man's cunning," said Kaa. "You are wise, but the Little People are always angry."

"No, at twilight all wings near and far rest for a while. I will play with the dhole at twilight, for the dhole hunts best by day. He follows Wontolla's blood-trail. Will you stay here, Kaa, till I come again with my dholes?"

"Yes, but what if they kill you in the Jungle, or the Little People kill you before you can leap down to the river?"

"When tomorrow comes we will kill for tomorrow," said Mowgli, quoting a Jungle saying. And again, "When I am dead it is time to sing the Death Song. Good hunting, Kaa!"

He loosened his arm from the python's neck and went down the gorge like a log in a freshet, paddling towards the far bank, where

he found slack-water, laughing aloud from sheer happiness.

He knew that the Little People hated the smell of wild garlic. So he gathered a small bundle of it, tied it up with a bark string, and then followed Won-tolla's blood-trail.

Won-tolla's trail, all rank with dark bloodspots, ran under a forest of thick trees that grew close together and stretched away north-eastward, gradually growing thinner and thinner to within two miles of the Bee Rocks. From the last tree to the low scrub of the Bee Rocks was open country, where there was hardly cover enough to hide a wolf. Mowgli trotted along under the trees, judging distances between branch and branch, occasionally climbing up a trunk and taking a trial leap from one tree to another till he came to the open ground, which he studied very carefully for an hour. Then he turned, picked up Won-tolla's trail where he had left it, settled himself in a tree

with an outrunning branch some eight feet from the ground, and sat still, sharpening his knife on the sole of his foot and singing to himself.

A little before mid-day, when the sun was very warm, he heard the patter of feet and smelt the abominable smell of the dhole-pack as they trotted pitilessly along Won-tolla's trail. Seen from above, the red dhole does not look half the size of a wolf, but Mowgli knew how strong his feet and jaws were. He watched the sharp bay head of the leader snuffing along the trail, and gave him "Good hunting!"

The brute looked up, and his companions halted behind him, scores and scores of red dogs with low-hung tails, heavy shoulders, weak quarters, and bloody mouths. The dholes are a very silent people as a rule, and they have no manners even in their own Jungle. Two hundred must have gathered below him, but he could see that the leaders sniffed hungrily on Won-tolla's trail, and tried to drag the Pack forward.

"By whose leave have you come here?" asked Mowgli.

"All Jungles are our Jungle," was the reply. Mowgli looked down with a smile, and imitated perfectly the sharp chitter-chatter of Chikai, the leaping rat of the Dekkan, meaning the dholes to understand that he considered them no better than Chikai. The Pack closed-up round the tree-trunk and the leader bayed savagely, calling Mowgli a tree-ape. For an answer Mowgli stretched down one naked leg and wriggled his bare toes just above the leader's head. That was more than enough to wake the Pack to stupid rage. Those who have hair between their toes do not care to be reminded of it. Mowgli said sweetly, "Dog, red dog! Go back to the Dekkan and eat lizards. Go to Chikai your brother— There is hair between every toe!" He twiddled his toes a second time.

"Come down before we starve you out, hairless ape!" yelled the Pack, and this was

exactly what Mowgli wanted. As Mowgli told Kaa, he had many little thorns under his tongue, and slowly and deliberately he drove the dholes from silence to growls, from growls to yells, and from yells to hoarse slavery ravings. They tried to answer his taunts, but a cub might as well have tried to answer Kaa in a rage, and all the while Mowgli's right hand lay crooked at his side, ready for action, his feet locked round the branch. The big bay leader had leaped many times in the air, but Mowgli dared not risk a false blow. At last, made furious beyond his natural strength, he bounded up seven or eight feet clear of the ground.

Then Mowgli's hand shot out like the head of a tree-snake, and gripped him by the scruff of his neck, and the branch shook with the jar as his weight fell back, almost wrenching Mowgli to the ground. Inch by inch he hauled the beast, hanging like a drowned jackal, up on the branch. With his left hand he reached for

his knife and cut off the red, bushy tail, flinging the dhole back to earth again. That was all he needed. The Pack would not go forward on Won-tolla's trail now till they had killed Mowgli or Mowgli had killed them. He saw them settle down in circles with a quiver of the haunches that meant they were going to stay, and so he climbed higher, settled his back comfortably, and went to sleep.

After three or four hours he woke up and counted the Pack. They were all there, silent, husky, and dry, with eyes of steel. The sun was beginning to sink. In half an hour the Little People of the Rocks would be ending their labours, and the dhole do not fight best in the twilight.

"I did not need such faithful watchers," he said politely, standing up on a branch, "but I will remember this."

"I myself will tear out your stomach!" yelled the leader, scratching at the foot of the tree.

"No, but consider, wise rat of the Dekkan. There will now be many litters of little tailless red dogs, with raw red stumps that sting when the sand is hot."

He moved, Bandar-log fashion, into the next tree, and so on into the next and the next, the Pack following with lifted hungry heads. Now and then he would pretend to fall, and the Pack would tumble one over the other in their haste to be at the death. It was a curious sight—the boy with the knife that shone in the low sunlight as it sifted through the upper branches, and the silent Pack with their red coats all aflame, huddling and following below. When he came to the last tree he took the garlic and rubbed himself all over carefully, and the dholes yelled with scorn.

"Ape with a wolf's tongue, are you trying to cover your scent? We follow to the death."

"Take your tail," said Mowgli, flinging it back along the course he had taken. The Pack

instinctively rushed after it. "And follow now —
to the death."

He had slipped down the tree-trunk, and
headed like the wind in bare feet for the Bee
Rocks, before the dholes saw what he would do.
They gave one deep howl, and settled down to
the long, lobbing canter that can at the last run
down anything that runs. Mowgli knew their
pack-pace was much slower than that of the
wolves, or he would never have risked a two
mile run in full sight. They were sure that the
boy was theirs at last, and he was sure that he
held them to play with as he pleased. All his
trouble was to keep them sufficiently hot behind
him to prevent their turning off too soon. He
ran cleanly, evenly with the tailless leader not
five yards behind him. The Little People had
gone to sleep in the early twilight, for it was
not the season of late blossoming flowers, but
as Mowgli's first footfalls rang hollow on the

hollow ground he heard a sound as though all the earth were humming.

Then he ran as he had never run in his life before, spurned aside one—two—three of the piles of stones into the dark, heard a roar like the roar of the sea in a cave, saw the air grow dark behind him, saw the current of the Waingunga far below and a flat, diamond-shaped head in the water. He leaped outward with all his strength, the tailless dhole snapping at his shoulder in mid-air, and dropped feet first to the safety of the river, breathless and triumphant. There was not a sting upon him, for the smell of the garlic had checked the Little People for just the few seconds that he was among them. When he rose Kaa's coils were steadying him and things were bounding over the edge of the cliff—great lumps, it seemed, of clustered bees falling like plummets; but before any lump touched water the bees flew upward and the body of a dhole whirled downstream.

Overhead they could hear furious short yells that were drowned in the roar of the wings of the Little People of the Rocks. A greater number of them, maddened by the stings, had flung themselves into the river; and, as Kaa said, the Waingunga was hungry water. Kaa held Mowgli fast till the boy had recovered his breath.

"We may not stay here," he said. "The Little People are angry indeed. Come!" Swimming low and diving as often as he could, Mowgli went down the river, knife in hand.

"Slowly, slowly," said Kaa. "One tooth does not kill a hundred unless it is a cobra's, and many of the dholes took water swiftly when they saw the Little People rise."

"The more work for my knife, then. How the Little People follow!" Mowgli sank again. The face of the water was blanketed with wild bees, buzzing sullenly and stinging all they found.

"Nothing was ever yet lost by silence," said Kaa — no sting could penetrate his scales — "just hear how they howl!"

Nearly half the pack had seen the trap their fellows rushed into, and turning sharp aside had flung themselves into the water where the gorge broke down in steep banks. Their cries of rage and their threats against the "tree-ape" who had brought them to their shame mixed with the yells and growls of those who had been punished by the Little People. To remain ashore was death, and every dhole knew it. Their pack was swept along the current, down to the deep eddies of the Peace Pool, but even there the angry Little People followed and forced them to the water again.

Mowgli could hear the voice of the tailless leader bidding his people hold on and kill out every wolf in Seeonee. But he did not waste his time in listening.

"One kills in the dark behind us!" snapped a dhole. Mowgli had dived forward like an otter, twitched a struggling dhole under water before he could open his mouth, and dark rings rose as the body plopped up, turning on its side. The dholes tried to turn, but the current prevented them, and the Little People darted at the heads and ears, and they could hear the challenge of the Seeonee Pack growing louder and deeper in the gathering darkness.

Again Mowgli dived, and again a dhole went under, and rose dead, and again the clamour broke out at the rear of the pack, some howling that it was best to go ashore, others calling on their leader to lead them back to the Dekkan, and others bidding Mowgli show himself and be killed.

A wolf came running along the bank on three legs, leaping up and down, laying his head sideways close to the ground, hunching his back, and breaking high into the air, as though he were playing with his cubs. It was Won-tolla, and he didn't say a word, but continued his horrible sport beside the dholes. They had been long in the water now, and were swimming wearily, their coats drenched and heavy, their bushy tails dragging like sponges, so tired and shaken that they, too, were silent, watching the pair of blazing eyes that moved abreast.

"Are you there, Man-cub?" said Won-tolla across the water.

"Ask of the dead, Outlier," Mowgli replied.

"Have none come downstream? I have tricked them in the broad daylight, and their leader lacks his tail, but here be some few for thee still. Where shall I drive them?"

"I will wait," said Won-tolla.

Nearer and nearer came the bay of the Seeonee wolves and a bend in the river drove the dholes forward among the sands and shoals opposite the Lairs. Then they saw their mistake. They should have landed half a mile higher up, and rushed the wolves on dry ground. Now it was too late. The bank was lined with burning

eyes, and except for the horrible pheeal that had never stopped since sundown, there was no sound in the Jungle. It seemed as though Wontolla were fawning on them to come ashore.

"Turn and take hold," said the leader of the dholes. The entire Pack flung themselves at the shore, threshing through the shoal water, till the face of the Waingunga was all white and torn, and the great ripples went from side to side, like bow-waves from a boat. Mowgli followed the rush, stabbing and slicing as the dholes, huddled together, rushed up the river beach in one wave.

Then the long fight began, for even now the dholes were two to one. But they met wolves fighting for all that made the Pack.

A wolf, you must know, flies at the throat, while a dhole, by preference, bites at the belly. So when the dholes were struggling out of the water and had to raise their heads, the odds were with the wolves. On dry land the wolves suffered. But in the water or ashore, Mowgli's

knife came and went without ceasing. Grey Brother, crouched between the boy's knees, was protecting his stomach, while the others guarded his back and either side, or stood over him when the shock of a leaping, yelling dhole who had thrown himself full on the steady blade bore him down. For the rest, it was one tangled confusion — a locked and swaying mob that moved from right to left and from left to right along the bank; and also ground round and round slowly on its own centre.

Once Mowgli passed Akela, a dhole on either flank, and his all but toothless jaws closed over the loins of a third, and once he saw Phao, his teeth set in the throat of a dhole, tugging the unwilling beast forward till the yearlings could finish him. But the bulk of the fight was blind flurry, hit, trip, and tumble, yelp, groan; behind him and above him. As the night wore on, Mowgli felt that the end was coming soon.

"The meat is very near the bone," Grey Brother yelled. He was bleeding from a score

of flesh wounds. Won-tolla was fearfully punished, but his grip had paralysed the dhole, who could not turn round and reach him.

"It is the tailless one!" said Mowgli, with a bitter laugh. And indeed it was the big bay-coloured leader. A dhole leaped to his leader's aid, but before his teeth had found Won-tolla's flank, Mowgli's knife was in his throat, and Grey Brother took what was left.

"And thus do we do in the Jungle," said Mowgli triumphantly.

The dhole shuddered, his head dropped, and he lay still, and Won-tolla dropped above him.

"The Blood Debt is paid," said Mowgli.

"He hunts no more," said Grey Brother," and Akela, too, is silent this long time."

Dhole after dhole was slinking away from those dark and bloody sands to the river, to the thick Jungle, upstream or downstream as he saw the road clear.

"The debt! The debt!" shouted Mowgli.

"Pay the debt! They have slain the Lone Wolf! Let not a dog go!"

He was flying to the river, knife in hand, to check any dhole who dared to take water, when, from under a mound of nine dead, rose Akela's head and forequarters, and Mowgli dropped on his knees beside the Lone Wolf.

Didn't I say it would be my last fight?" Akela gasped. "It is good hunting. And you, Little Brother?"

"I live, having killed many."

"I die, and I would—I would die by you, Little Brother."

Mowgli took the terrible scarred head on his knees, and put his arms round the torn neck.

"It is long since the old days of Shere Khan, and a Man-cub that rolled naked in the dust."

"I am a wolf. I am of one skin with the Free People," Mowgli cried. "It is not my choice that I am a man."

"You are a man, Little Brother. I owe my life to you and today you have saved the Pack. All

194

debts are paid now. Go to your own people. This hunting is ended. Go to your own people."

"I will never go, I will hunt alone in the Jungle. I have said it."

"After the summer come the Rains, and after the Rains comes the spring. Go back before you are driven away."

"Who will drive me away?"

"Mowgli will drive Mowgli. Go back to your people. Go to Man."

"When Mowgli drives Mowgli I will go," Mowgli answered.

"There is no more to say," said Akela. "Little Brother, can you help me rise to my feet? I also was a leader of the Free People."

Very carefully and gently Mowgli lifted the bodies aside, and raised Akela to his feet, both arms round him, and the Lone Wolf drew a long breath, and began the Death Song that a leader of the Pack should sing when he dies. It gathered strength as he went on lifting and lifting, and ringing far across the river, till it

came to the last "Good hunting!" and Akela shook himself clear of Mowgli for an instant, and, leaping into the air, fell backward dead upon his last and most terrible kill.

Mowgli sat with his head on his knees, careless of anything else, while the remnant of the flying dholes were being overtaken and run down by the merciless lahinis. Little by little the cries died away, and the wolves returned limping, as their wounds stiffened, to take stock of the losses.

And Mowgli sat through it all till the cold daybreak, when Phao's wet, red muzzle was dropped in his hand, and Mowgli drew back to show the gaunt body of Akela.

"Good hunting!" said Phao, as though Akela were still alive. But of all the Pack of 200 fighting dholes, whose boast was that all Jungles were their Jungle, and that no living thing could stand before them, not one returned to the Dekkan to carry that word.

Chapter Six

The Spring Running

Mowgli could stop a young buck in mid-gallop and throw him sideways by the head. He could even jerk over the big, blue wild boars that lived in the Marshes of the North. The Jungle People who used to fear him for his wits feared him now for his strength, and when he moved quietly on his own affairs the mere whisper of his coming cleared the wood-paths. And yet the look in his eyes was always gentle. Even when he fought, his eyes never blazed as Bagheera's did. They only grew more and more interested and excited; and that was one of the things that Bagheera himself did not understand.

He asked Mowgli about it, and the boy laughed and said, "When I miss the kill I am angry. When I must go empty for two days I am very angry. Do not my eyes talk then?"

"The mouth is hungry," said Bagheera, "but the eyes say nothing. Hunting, eating, or swimming, it is all one—like a stone in wet or dry weather."

Mowgli looked at him lazily from under his long eyelashes, and as usual, the panther's head dropped. Bagheera knew his master. They were lying out far up the side of a hill overlooking the Waingunga, and the morning mists hung below them in bands of white and green. As the sun rose it changed into bubbling seas of red gold, churned off, and let the low rays stripe the dried grass on which Mowgli and Bagheera were resting.

"It was the end of the cold weather, the leaves and the trees looked worn and faded, and there was a dry, ticking rustle everywhere

when the wind blew. A little leaf tap-tapped furiously against a twig, as a single leaf caught in a current will. It roused Bagheera, for he snuffed the morning air with a deep, hollow cough, threw himself on his back, and struck with his fore-paws at the nodding leaf above.

"The year turns," he said. "The Jungle goes forward. The Time of New Talk is near. That leaf knows. It is very good."

"The grass is dry," Mowgli answered, pulling up a tuft. "Even Eye-of-the-Spring (that is a little trumpet-shaped, waxy red flower that runs in and out among the grasses) and . . . Bagheera, is it well for the Black Panther so to lie on his back and beat with his paws in the air, as though he were the tree cat?"

"Aowh?" said Bagheera. He seemed to be thinking of other things.

"I say, is it well for the Black Panther so to mouth and cough, and howl and roll? Remember, we are the Masters of the Jungle, you and I."

"Indeed, yes, I hear, Man-cub." Bagheera rolled over hurriedly and sat up, the dust on his ragged black flanks (He was just casting his winter coat).

"We are surely the Masters of the Jungle! Who is as strong as Mowgli? Who so wise?" There was a curious drawl in the voice that made Mowgli turn to see whether by any chance the Black Panther were making fun of him, for the Jungle is full of words that sound like one thing, but mean another.

"I said we are beyond question the Masters of the Jungle," Bagheera repeated. "Have I done something wrong? I did not know that the Man-cub no longer lay upon the ground. Does he fly, then?"

Mowgli sat with his elbows on his knees, looking out across the valley at the daylight. Somewhere down in the woods below a bird was trying over in a husky, reedy voice the first few notes of his spring song.

"I said the Time of New Talk is near," growled the panther, switching his tail. That is what the Jungle People called the Spring.

"I hear," Mowgli answered. "Bagheera, why are you shaking all over? The sun is warm?"

"That is Ferao, the scarlet woodpecker," said Bagheera. "He has not forgotten. Now I, too, must remember my song," and he began purring and crooning to himself, harking back dissatisfied again and again.

"I had forgotten. I shall know when the Time of New Talk is here, because then you and the others all run away and leave me alone," Mowgli spoke rather savagely.

"But, Little Brother," Bagheera began, "we do not always."

"You do," said Mowgli, shooting out his forefinger angrily. "You do run away, and I, who am the Master of the Jungle, has to walk alone. How was it last season, when I would gather sugarcane from the fields of a Man-Pack. I sent you to Hathi, bidding him to come at night and pluck the sweet grass for me with his trunk."

"He came only two nights later," said Bagheera, cowering a little, "and of that long, sweet grass that pleased thee so he gathered more than any Man-cub could eat in all the nights of the Rains. That was no fault of mine."

"He did not come upon the night when I sent for him. No, he was trumpeting and running and roaring through the valleys in the moonlight. His trail was like the trail of three elephants, for he would not hide among the trees. He danced in the moonlight before the houses of the Man-Pack. I saw him, and yet he would not come to me, and *I* am the Master of the Jungle!"

"Perhaps, Little Brother, you did not that time call him by a Master-word? Listen to Ferao, and be glad!"

Mowgli's bad temper seemed to have boiled itself away. He lay back with his head on his arms, his eyes shut. "I do not know — nor do I care," he

said sleepily. "Let us sleep, Bagheera. My stomach is heavy in me. Make me a rest for my head."

The panther lay down again with a sigh, because he could hear Ferao practising and repractising his song against the Springtime of New Talk, as they say. In an Indian Jungle the seasons slide one into the other almost without division. There seem to be only two—the wet and the dry. But if you look closely below the torrents of rain and the clouds of dust you will find all four going round in their regular ring.

There is one day when all things are tired, and the very smells, as they drift on the heavy air, are old and used. One cannot explain this, but it feels so. Then there is another day—to the eye nothing whatever has changed—when all the smells are new and delightful, and the whiskers of the Jungle People quiver to their roots, and the winter hair comes away from their sides in long, draggled locks. Then, perhaps, a little rain falls, and all the trees and

the bushes wake with a noise of growing that you can almost hear, and under this noise runs, day and night, a deep hum. That is the noise of the spring—a vibrating boom which is neither bees, nor falling water, nor the wind in tree-tops, but the purring of the warm, happy world. Up to this year Mowgli had always delighted in the turn of the seasons. It was he who generally saw the first Eye-of-the-Spring deep down among the grasses, and the first bank of spring clouds, which are like nothing else in the Jungle.

Like all his people, spring was the season he chose for his Sittings—moving, for the mere joy of rushing through the warm air, 30, 40 or 50 miles between twilight and the morning star, and coming back panting and laughing and wreathed with strange flowers. The Four did not follow him on these wild ringings of the Jungle, but went off to sing songs with other wolves. The Jungle People are very busy in the spring, and Mowgli could hear them grunting

and screaming and whistling according to their kind. Their voices then are different from their voices at other times of the year, and that is one of the reasons why spring in the Jungle is called the Time of New Talk.

But that spring, as he told Bagheera, his stomach was changed in him. Ever since the bamboo shoots turned spotty-brown he had been looking forward to the morning when the smells should change. But when the morning came, and Mor the Peacock, blazing in bronze and blue and gold, cried it aloud all along the misty woods, and Mowgli opened his mouth to send on the cry, the words choked between his teeth, and a feeling came over him that began at his toes and ended in his hair—a feeling of pure unhappiness, so that he looked himself over to be sure that he had not trod on a thorn, Mor cried the new smells, the other birds took it over, and from the rocks by the Waingunga he heard Bagheera's hoarse scream— something

between the scream of an eagle and the neighing of a horse. There was a yelling and scattering of Bandar-log in the new-budding branches above and there stood Mowgli, his chest, filled to answer Mor, sinking in little gasps as the breath was driven out of it by this unhappiness.

He stared all around him, but he could see no more than the mocking Bandar-log scudding through the trees, and Mor, his tail spread in full splendour, dancing on the slopes below.

A light spring rain—elephant-rain they call it—drove across the Jungle in a belt half a mile wide, left the new leaves wet and nodding behind, and died out in a double rainbow and a light roll of thunder. The spring hum broke out for a minute, and was silent, but all the Jungle Folk seemed to be giving tongue at once. All except Mowgli.

"I have eaten good food," he said to himself. "I have drunk good water. Nor does my throat burn and grow small, as it did when I bit the blue-spotted root that Oo the Turtle said was clean food. But my stomach is heavy, and I have given very bad talk to Bagheera and others, people of the Jungle and my people. Now, too, I am hot and now I am cold, and now I am neither hot nor cold, but angry with that which I cannot see. It is time to make a running! Tonight I will cross the ranges, yes, I will make a spring running to the Marshes of the North, and back again. I have hunted too easily too long. The Four shall come with me, for they grow fat."

He called, but never one of the Four answered.

They were far beyond earshot, singing over the spring songs—the Moon and Sambhur Songs—with the wolves of the Pack; for in the spring-time the Jungle People make very little difference between the day and the night. He gave the sharp, barking note, but his only answer was the mocking maiou of the little spotted tree-cat winding in and out among the branches for early birds' nests. At this he shook all over with rage, and half drew his knife. Then he became very haughty, though there was no one to see him, and stalked severely down the hillside, chin up and eyebrows down. But never a single one of his people asked him a question, for they were all too busy with their own affairs.

"Yes," said Mowgli to himself, though in his heart he knew that he had no reason. "Let the Red Dhole come from the Dekkan, or the Red Flower dance among the bamboos, and all the Jungle runs whining to Mowgli, calling him great elephant-names. But now, because Eye-of-the Spring is red, and Mor, must show his naked legs in some spring dance, the Jungle goes mad. Am I the Master of the Jungle, or am I not?"

A couple of young wolves of the Pack were cantering down a path, looking for open ground in which to fight. (You will remember that the Law of the Jungle forbids fighting where the Pack can see.) Their neck-bristles were as stiff as wire, and they bayed furiously, crouching

for the first grapple. Mowgli leaped forward, caught one outstretched throat in either hand, expecting to fling the creatures backward as he had often done in games or Pack hunts. But he had never before interfered with a spring fight. The two leaped forward and dashed him aside, and without word to waste rolled over and over. Mowgli was on his feet almost before he fell, his knife and his white teeth were bared. He danced round them with lowered shoulders and quivering hand, ready to send in a double blow when the first flurry of the scuffle should be over; but while he waited the strength seemed to ebb from his body, the knife-point lowered, and he sheathed the knife and watched.

"I have surely eaten poison," he sighed at last. "My strength is gone from me, and presently I shall die. The fight went on till one wolf ran away, and Mowgli was left alone on the torn and bloody ground, looking now at his knife, and now at his legs and arms, while

the feeling of unhappiness he had never known before covered him as water covers a log.

He killed early that evening and ate little, and he ate alone because all the Jungle People were away singing or fighting. He was so unhappy that it frightened him.

He was so sorry for himself that he nearly wept. "And after," he went on, "they will find me lying in the black water. No, I will go back to my own Jungle, and I will die upon the Council Rock, and Bagheera, whom I love, if he is not screaming in the valley. A large, warm tear splashed down on his knee. He was quiet for a little, thinking of the last words of the Lone Wolf, which you, of course, remember.

"Now Akela said to me many foolish things before he died, for when we die our stomachs change. He said … None the less, I *am* of the Jungle!"

"I will look," said he, "as I did in the old days, and I will see how far the Man-Pack has changed."

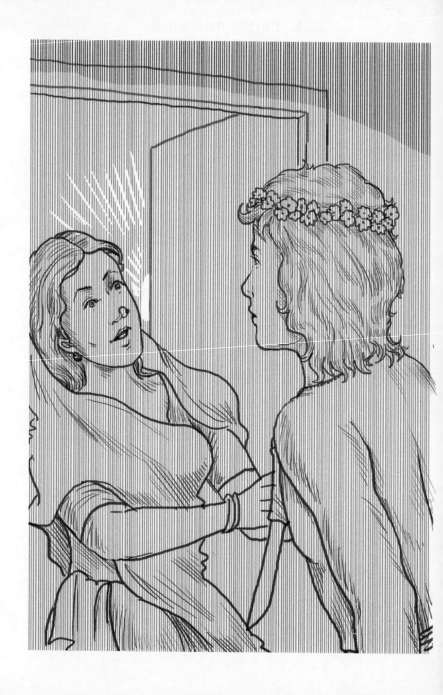

Forgetting that he was no longer in his own Jungle, where he could do what he pleased, he trod carelessly through the dew-loaded grasses till he came to the hut where the light stood. Three or four yelping dogs barked, for he was on the outskirts of a village.

The door of the hut opened, and a woman stood peering out into the darkness. A child cried, and the woman said something over her shoulder.

Mowgli in the grass began to shake as though he had fever. He knew that voice well, but to make sure he cried softly, surprised to find how man's talk came back, "Messua! O Messua!"

"Who is it?" said the woman, a quiver in her voice.

"Have you forgotten?" said Mowgli. His throat was dry as he spoke. "I am Nathoo!" said Mowgli, for, as you remember, that was the name Messua gave him when he first came to the Man-Pack.

"Come, my son," she called, and Mowgli stepped into the light, and looked full at Messua, the woman who had been good to him, and whose life he had saved from the Man-Pack so long before. She was older, and her hair was grey, but her eyes and her voice had not changed. Woman-like, she expected to find Mowgli where she had left him, and her eyes travelled upward in a puzzled way from his chest to his head, that touched the top of the door.

"My son," she stammered, and then, sinking to his feet, "but it is no longer my son. It is a Godling of the Woods! Ahai!"

As he stood in the red light of the oil-lamp, strong, tall and beautiful, his long black hair sweeping over his shoulders, the knife swinging at his neck, and his head crowned with a wreath of white jasmine, he might easily have been mistaken for some wild god of a jungle legend. The child half asleep on a cot sprang up and shrieked aloud with terror. Messua turned to soothe him, while Mowgli stood still looking in at the water-jars and the cooking-pots, the grain-bin, and all the other human belongings that he found himself remembering so well.

"I did not know you were here. Where is your husband and who is that child?"

"This is my son, born two years ago. His father died last year. Would you bless this child, so that he may be safe among your people of the Jungle?"

Mowgli sat down, muttering, with his face in his hands. All manner of strange feelings that he had never felt before were running over him, exactly as though he had been poisoned, and he felt dizzy and a little sick. He drank the warm milk Messua gave him in long gulps, with her patting him on the shoulder from time to time, not quite sure whether he were her son Nathoo of the long ago days, or some wonderful Jungle being, but glad to feel that he was at least flesh and blood.

"Son," she said at last, her eyes were full of pride, "has anyone told you that you are beautiful beyond all men?"

"Hah?" said Mowgli, for naturally he had never heard anything of the kind. Messua laughed softly and happily. The look in his face was enough for her.

"I am the first, then? You are very beautiful. Never have I looked upon such a man."

Mowgli twisted his head and tried to see over his own hard shoulder, and Messua laughed again so long that Mowgli, not knowing why, was forced to laugh with her, and the child ran from one to the other, laughing too.

Mowgli could not understand one word in three of the talk here; the warm milk was taking effect on him after his long run, so he curled up and in a minute was deep asleep, and Messua put the hair back from his eyes, threw a cloth over him, and was happy. Jungle-fashion, he slept out the rest of that night and all the next day, for his instincts, which never wholly slept, warned him there was nothing to fear. He woke up at last with a bound that shook the hut, for the cloth over his face made him dream of traps; and there he stood, his hand on his knife, the sleep all heavy in his rolling eyes, ready for any fight. Messua laughed, and set the evening meal before him.

Messua also insisted that his hair must be cleaned out. So she sang, as she combed, foolish little baby-songs, now calling Mowgli her son, and now begging him to give some of his jungle power to the child. The hut door was closed, but Mowgli heard a sound he knew well, and saw Messua's jaw drop with horror as a great grey paw came under the bottom of the door, and Grey Brother outside whined a muffled and penitent whine of anxiety and fear.

"Wait outside! You did not come when I called," said Mowgli in Jungle-talk, without turning his head, and the great grey paw disappeared. Mother, I am going."

Messua drew aside humbly — he was indeed a wood-god, she thought, but as his hand was on the door the mother in her made her throw her arms round Mowgli's neck again and again.

"Come back!" she whispered. "Son or no son, come back, for I love you. By night or by day this door is never shut to you."

The child was crying because the man with the shiny knife was going away. Mowgli met Grey Brother outside.

"O Little Brother, what hast *thou* done, eating and sleeping with the Man-Pack?"

"If you had come when I called, this would have never been," said Mowgli, running much faster.

"And now what is to be?" asked Grey Brother.

Mowgli was going to answer when a girl in a white cloth came down some path that led from the outskirts of the village. Grey Brother dropped out of sight at once, and Mowgli backed noiselessly into a field of high-springing

crops. He could almost have touched her with his hand when the warm, green stalks closed before his face and he disappeared like a ghost. The girl screamed, for she thought she had seen a spirit, and then she gave a deep sigh. Mowgli parted the stalks with his hands and watched her till she was out of sight.

"And now I do not know," he said, sighing in his turn. "*Why* did you not come when I called?"

"We follow you always."

"And would you follow me to the Man-Pack?" Mowgli whispered. "Again and again, and it may be again."

Grey Brother was silent. When he spoke he growled to himself, "The Black One spoke truth."

"What did he say?"

"Man goes *to* Man at the last. Raksha, our mother, said the same."

"And so said Akela on the night of Red Dog," Mowgli muttered.

The Four looked at one another and at Mowgli, puzzled but obedient.

"The Jungle does not cast me out, then?" Mowgli stammered.

Grey Brother and the Three growled furiously, beginning, "So long as we live none shall dare—"

But Baloo stopped them. "I taught you the Jungle Law," he said, "and, though I cannot now see the rocks before me, *I* see far. Little Frog, take your own trail, make your lair with your own blood and pack and people, but when there is need of foot or tooth or eye, or a word carried swiftly by night, remember, Master of the Jungle, the Jungle is yours at call."

"The Middle Jungle is yours also," said Kaa. "I speak for no small people."

"My brothers," cried Mowgli, throwing up his arms with a sob. "I know not what I know! I would not go, but I am drawn by both feet. How shall I leave these nights?"

"No, look up. Little Brother," Baloo repeated. "There is no shame in this hunting. When the honey is eaten we leave the empty hive."

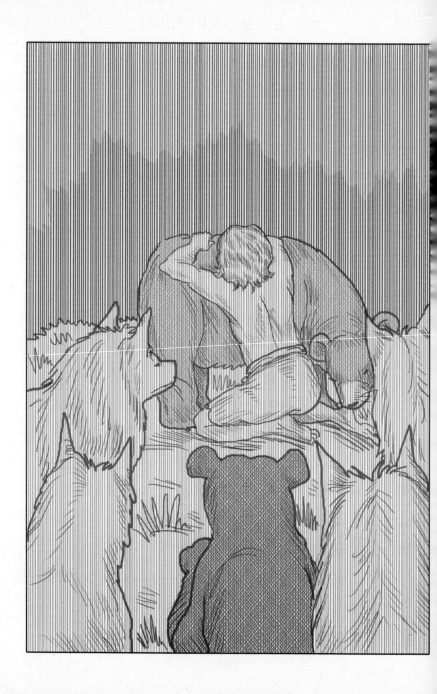

"Having cast the skin," said Kaa, "we may not creep into it afresh. It is the Law."

"Listen, dearest of all to me," said Baloo. "There is neither word nor will here to hold you back. Look up! Who may question the Master of the Jungle?"

"I saw you playing among the white pebbles there when you were a little frog and so did Bagheera. Everyone else from that time is dead."

Mowgli sobbed and sobbed, with his head on the blind bear's side and his arms round his neck, while Baloo tried feebly to lick his feet.

"The stars are thin," said Grey Brother, snuffing at the dawn wind. "Where shall we lair today? For, from now, we follow new trails."

And this is the last of the Mowgli stories.

About The Author

■ Rudyard Kipling

Joseph Rudyard Kipling (1865-1936) was born in the Bombay of British India and only moved to England when he was five years old. He graduated from the United Services College in north Devon. His father, John Lockwood Kipling, was an artist and was the principal of the Jeejeebyhoy Art School. He returned to India in 1882, where he worked for Anglo-Indian newspapers. He was an English short-story writer, poet and novelist. He is chiefly remembered for his stories and poems of British soldiers in India and his tales for children. Kipling is best known for his works of fiction, including *The Jungle Book* (1894), which is a much loved children's classic across the world. He also wrote *Second Jungle Book* (1895), *Just So Stories* (1902), and many other short stories. His other very celebrated work is *Kim* (1901).

He was awarded the Nobel Prize in Literature in 1907, making him the first English-language writer to receive the prize, and to date he remains its youngest recipient. He received the Gold Medal of the Royal Society of Literature in 1926 among other honours.

He died in London on 18 January 1936, just after his 70th birthday, and was buried in Westminster Abbey. The following year saw the posthumous publication of his autobiography *Something of Myself*.

■ Characters

Mowgli - The man-cub, who was abducted by Shere Khan from the local village, was raised by a family of wolves in the Indian jungle. He was trained by the friendly bear Baloo and guided through his life in the jungle by Bagheera, a black panther. He fights Shere Khan and kills him, showing remarkable courage and presence of mind. Mowgli was a loyal friend to Akela, the old lone wolf, till the end.

Baloo - Baloo, the bear, is Mowgli's friend, philosopher and guide in the jungle. He, along with Bagheera had stood up for Mowgli, when the Wolf Pack had cast him off.

Bagheera - Although not as dedicated as Baloo in teaching Mowgli the laws of the jungle, Bagheera, the black panther, is responsible in many ways for bringing up Mowgli. He helps Mowgli to fight Shere Khan at every step.

Shere Khan - The villain of the story, Shere Khan is a lame tiger, who hunts cattle from the nearby village. He had kidnapped Mowgli from the village to make him his prey, but the child escaped into the cave of a family of wolves. Shere Khan tried repeatedly to replace Akela as the leader of the Wolf Pack and to make Mowgli his food. In the end, he was killed by Mowgli with the help of his friends.

Kaa - Kaa, the rock python, helped Bagheera and Baloo in rescuing Mowgli from Bandar Log. Kaa also helps Mowgli defend the Jungle from the Dhole and later leads him to the vast treasure of the lost ancient kingdom.

Akela - The lone old wolf, Akela, was the leader of the Wolf Pack. He accepted Mowgli into their pack. When he grew old, Shere Khan tried to replace him as the leader of the pack, but Mowgli managed to scare Shere Khan away. Akela helps Mowgli to trap Shere Khan in the village with the buffalo herds and kill him.

Raksha - Raksha is the Mother Wolf, who brought Mowgli up along with her cubs. She displayed immense courage by standing up to Shere Khan and the wolf pack and adopting Mowgli. She named Mowgli after a frog.

Gray Brother - The oldest of Father Wolf and Raksha's cubs helps Mowgli kill Shere Khan.

Messua - Messua is the wife of the richest man of the human village, who provides food and shelter to Mowgli, believing (probably mistakenly) him to be her long-lost son Nathoo.

Buldeo - Buldeo is the village hunter who is boastful and arrogant. He gets furious when Mowgli contradicts some of his fanciful stories about the jungle. He tries to turn the village against Mowgli when Mowgli kills Shere Khan.

Purun Dass- Purun Das is a prominent and successful civil servant of British India. He is popular and uses his position to change many lives for the better. One fine day he decides to renounce everything and goes and starts living at a Kali temple in the mountains. He also starts calling himself Purun Bhagat.

The White Cobra- The white cobra is an ancient cobra who still believes he protects the king's treasure from robbers. He is unaware that the Jungle had taken over the city.

▪ Questions

Chapter 1
- *Why was the Law of the Jungle important?*
- *Who taught Mowgli about the Law? What did he compare it to?*
- *How did the Forest dry up?*

- *What did the residents of the Jungle do?*
- *How did Mowgli and his friends spend their days in the heat?*
- *What was the 'Water truce'?*
- *What story did Hathi tell?*
- *Why had Baloo not told Mowgli the story before?*

Chapter 2

- *Who was Purun Dass?*
- *Why did Purun Dass work with the British rule?*
- *What strange thing did Purun Dass do?*
- *What was Purun Dass's new name? Where did travel to?*
- *What did the villagers do when they saw Purun Bhagat?*
- *Who were Purun Bhagat's closest friends?*
- *What did Bara Singh wake Purun in the middle of the night?*
- *How did the villagers remember Purun Bhagat?*

Chapter 3

- *What did Mowgli and his Wolf family talk about?*
- *What did Mowgli decide they should do with the man in the forest?*
- *Who sang the forest song?*
- *What did Messua tell Mowgli? Who was she?*
- *Why had the villagers turned against Messua and her husband?*
- *What did Mowgli and Mother Wolf talk about?*
- *How did Mowgli ensure Messua's safety?*
- *What master word did Mowgli have for Hathi?*
- *What did Mowgli ask Hathi to do?*
- *How did Hathi accomplish his Mowgli's work?*

Chapter 4

- *What was the regular game between Kaa and Mowgli?*
- *Who were the Poison people?*

- *Where did Kaa take Mowgli?*
- *What happened when they met the Cobra?*
- *Where had the cobra belonged? What did the cobra guard?*
- *Why did Mowgli decide that the Cobra was harmless?*
- *What did Mowgli take from the cave?*
- *What made Mowgli return it?*
- *What did he tell the Cobra when he left?*

Chapter 5
- *How did Mowgli's life in the Jungle change as the others grew old?*
- *What danger approached the Jungle?*
- *How did Mowgli plan for the fight?*
- *How did he trap the Dhole?*
- *Where did Mowgli lead the Dhole pack to?*
- *What happened during the battle?*
- *What did Akela tell Mowgli as he died?*

Chapter 6
- *What was the spring running?*
- *Why did Mowgli feel so lonely?*
- *What did Mowgli do when he felt lonely?*
- *What did Messua say to Mowgli?*
- *Who was the child? What had happened to his father?*
- *How did Messua treat Mowgli?*
- *What did Mowgli talk about with the Jungle people when he returned?*
- *What did Mowgli decide about where his home was going to be?*